Matthew Ar

Poems

SALZWASSER
VERLAG

Matthew Arnold

Poems

1st Edition | ISBN: 978-3-75250-224-4

Place of Publication: Frankfurt am Main, Germany

Year of Publication: 2020

Salzwasser Verlag GmbH, Germany.

Reprint of the original, first published in 1869.

POEMS

DRAMATIC AND LYRIC

POEMS

BY

MATTHEW ARNOLD

THE SECOND VOLUME

DRAMATIC AND LYRIC POEMS

London

MACMILLAN AND CO.

M DCCC LXIX

CONTENTS.

vi CONTENTS.

Though the Muse be gone away,
Though she move not earth to-day,
Souls, erewhile who caught her word,
Ah! still harp on what they heard.

EMPEDOCLES ON ETNA.

A DRAMATIC POEM.

EMPEDOCLES ON ETNA.

ACT I, SCENE I.

A Pass in the forest region of Etna.   Morning.

CALLICLES.

(Alone, resting on a rock by the path.)

THE mules, I think, will not be here this hour!
  They feel the cool wet turf under their feet
By the stream-side, after the dusty lanes
In which they have toil'd all night from Catana,
And scarcely will they budge a yard.   O Pan!
How gracious is the mountain at this hour!
A thousand times have I been here alone
Or with the revellers from the mountain-towns,
But never on so fair a morn!—the sun
Is shining on the brilliant mountain-crests,
And on the highest pines; but farther down
Here in the valley is in shade; the sward
Is dark, and on the stream the mist still hangs;

One sees one's foot-prints crush'd in the wet grass,
One's breath curls in the air; and on these pines
That climb from the stream's edge, the long grey tufts,
Which the goats love, are jewell'd thick with dew.
Here will I stay till the slow litter comes.
I have my harp too—that is well.—Apollo!
What mortal could be sick or sorry here?
I know not in what mind Empedocles,
Whose mules I follow'd, may be coming up,
But if, as most men say, he is half mad
With exile, and with brooding on his wrongs,
Pausanias, his sage friend, who mounts with him,
Could scarce have lighted on a lovelier cure.
The mules must be below, far down. I hear
Their tinkling bells, mix'd with the song of birds,
Rise faintly to me—now it stops!—Who's here?
Pausanias! and on foot? alone?

Pausanias.

And thou, then?
I left thee supping with Peisianax,
With thy head full of wine, and thy hair crown'd,
Touching thy harp as the whim came on thee,
And praised and spoil'd by master and by guests

Almost as much as the new dancing girl.
Why hast thou follow'd us?

Callicles.

              The night was hot,
And the feast past its prime; so we slipp'd out,
Some of us, to the portico to breathe;—
Peisianax, thou know'st, drinks late;—and then,
As I was lifting my soil'd garland off,
I saw the mules and litter in the court,
And in the litter sate Empedocles;
Thou, too, wast with him. Straightway I sped home;
I saddled my white mule, and all night long
Through the cool lovely country follow'd you,
Pass'd you a little since as morning dawn'd,
And have this hour sate by the torrent here,
Till the slow mules should climb in sight again.
And now?

Pausanias.

        And now, back to the town with speed!
Crouch in the wood first, till the mules have pass'd;
They do but halt, they will be here anon.
Thou must be viewless to Empedocles!

Save mine, he must not meet a human eye.
One of his moods is on him that thou know'st;
I think, thou wouldst not vex him.

Callicles.

                         No—and yet
I would fain stay and help thee tend him! once
He knew me well, and would oft notice me.
And still, I know not how, he draws me to him,
And I could watch him with his proud sad face,
His flowing locks and gold-encircled brow
And kingly gait, for ever; such a spell
In his severe looks, such a majesty
As drew of old the people after him,
In Agrigentum and Olympia,
When his star reign'd, before his banishment,
Is potent still on me in his decline.
But oh, Pausanias, he is changed of late!
There is a settled trouble in his air
Admits no momentary brightening now;
And when he comes among his friends at feasts,
'Tis as an orphan among prosperous boys.
Thou know'st of old he loved this harp of mine,
When first he sojourn'd with Peisianax;

He is now always moody, and I fear him;
But I would serve him, soothe him, if I could,   ,
Dared one but try.

Pausanias.

Thou wast a kind child ever!
He loves thee, but he must not see thee now.
Thou hast indeed a rare touch on thy harp,
He loves that in thee, too—there was a time
(But that is pass'd) he would have paid thy strain
With music to have drawn the stars from heaven.
He has his harp and laurel with him still,
But he has laid the use of music by,
And all which might relax his settled gloom.
Yet thou may'st try thy playing if thou wilt—
But thou must keep unseen; follow us on,
But at a distance; in these solitudes,
In this clear mountain-air, a voice will rise,
Though from afar, distinctly; it may soothe him.
Play when we halt, and, when the evening comes
And I must leave him (for his pleasure is
To be left musing these soft nights alone
In the high unfrequented mountain-spots),
Then watch him, for he ranges swift and far,

Sometimes to Etna's top, and to the cone;
But hide thee in the rocks a great way down,
And try thy noblest strains, my Callicles,
With the sweet night to help thy harmony!
Thou wilt earn my thanks sure, and perhaps his.

Callicles.

More than a day and night, Pausanias,
Of this fair summer weather, on these hills,
Would I bestow to help Empedocles!
That needs no thanks; one is far better here
Than in the broiling city in these heats.
But tell me, how hast thou persuaded him
In this his present fierce, man-hating mood,
To bring thee out with him alone on Etna?

Pausanias.

Thou hast heard all men speaking of Pantheia,
The woman who at Agrigentum lay
Thirty long days in a cold trance of death,
And whom Empedocles call'd back to life.
Thou art too young to note it, but his power
Swells with the swelling evil of this time,
And holds men mute to see where it will rise.

He could stay swift diseases in old days,
Chain madmen by the music of his lyre,
Cleanse to sweet airs the breath of poisonous streams,
And in the mountain-chinks inter the winds.
This he could do of old; but now, since all
Clouds and grows daily worse in Sicily,
Since broils tear us in twain, since this new swarm
Of sophists has got empire in our schools
Where he was paramount, since he is banish'd,
And lives a lonely man in triple gloom,
He grasps the very reins of life and death.
I ask'd him of Pantheia yesterday,
When we were gather'd with Peisianax,
And he made answer, I should come at night
On Etna here, and be alone with him,
And he would tell me, as his old, tried friend,
Who still was faithful, what might profit me;
That is, the secret of this miracle.

Callicles.

Bah! Thou a doctor! Thou art superstitious.
Simple Pausanias, 'twas no miracle!
Pantheia, for I know her kinsmen well,
Was subject to these trances from a girl.

Empedocles would say so, did he deign;
But he still lets the people, whom he scorns,
Gape and cry wizard at him, if they list.
But thou, thou art no company for him!
Thou art as cross, as soured as himself.
Thou hast some wrong from thine own citizens,
And then thy friend is banish'd, and on that,
Straightway thou fallest to arraign the times,
As if the sky was impious not to fall.
The sophists are no enemies of his;
I hear, Gorgias, their chief, speaks nobly of him,
As of his gifted master and once friend.
He is too scornful, too high-wrought, too bitter!
'Tis not the times, 'tis not the sophists vex him;
There is some root of suffering in himself,
Some secret and unfollow'd vein of woe,
Which makes the time look black and sad to him.
Pester him not in this his sombre mood
With questionings about an idle tale;
But lead him through the lovely mountain-paths,
And keep his mind from preying on itself,
And talk to him of things at hand and common,
Not miracles! thou art a learned man,
But credulous of fables as a girl.

Pausanias.

And thou, a boy whose tongue outruns his knowledge,
And on whose lightness blame is thrown away.
Enough of this! I see the litter wind
Up by the torrent-side, under the pines.
I must rejoin Empedocles. Do thou
Crouch in the brushwood till the mules have pass'd;
Then play thy kind part well. Farewell till night!

SCENE II.

Noon. A Glen on the highest skirts of the woody region of Etna.

EMPEDOCLES. PAUSANIAS.

Pausanias.

THE noon is hot! when we have cross'd the stream,
We shall have left the woody tract, and come
Upon the open shoulder of the hill.
See how the giant spires of yellow bloom
Of the sun-loving gentian, in the heat,[1]
Are shining on those naked slopes like flame!
Let us rest here; and now, Empedocles,
Pantheia's history!

[*A harp-note below is heard.*

Empedocles.

                    Hark! what sound was that
Rose from below? If it were possible,
And we were not so far from human haunt,
I should have said that some one touch'd a harp.
Hark! there again!

Pausanias.

'Tis the boy Callicles,
The sweetest harp-player in Catana !
He is for ever coming on these hills,
In summer, to all country-festivals,
With a gay revelling band; he breaks from them
Sometimes, and wanders far among the glens.
But heed him not, he will not mount to us;
I spoke with him this morning. Once more, therefore,
Instruct me of Pantheia's story, Master,
As I have pray'd thee.

Empedocles.

That? and to what end?

Pausanias.

It is enough that all men speak of it.
But I will also say, that when the Gods
Visit us as they do with sign and plague,
To know those spells of thine that stay their hand
Were to live free from terror.

Empedocles.

Spells? Mistrust them!
Mind is the spell which governs earth and heaven;

Man has a mind with which to plan his safety—
Know that, and help thyself!

Pausanias.

                But thy own words?
' The wit and counsel of man was never clear,
Troubles confuse the little wit he has.'
Mind is a light which the Gods mock us with,
To lead those false who trust it.

                [*The harp sounds again.*

Empedocles.

                Hist! once more!
Listen, Pausanias!—Ay, 'tis Callicles!
I know those notes among a thousand.   Hark!

Callicles.

(*Sings unseen, from below.*)

The track winds down to the clear stream
To cross the sparkling shallows; there
The cattle love to gather, on their way
To the high mountain-pastures, and to stay,
Till the rough cow-herds drive them past,
Knee-deep in the cool ford; for 'tis the last

Of all the woody, high, well-water'd dells
On Etna; and the beam
Of noon is broken there by chestnut-boughs
Down its steep verdant sides; the air
Is freshen'd by the leaping stream, which throws
Eternal showers of spray on the moss'd roots
Of trees, and veins of turf, and long dark shoots
Of ivy-plants, and fragrant hanging bells
Of hyacinths, and on late anemonies,
That muffle its wet banks; but glade,
And stream, and sward, and chestnut-trees,
End here; Etna beyond, in the broad glare
Of the hot noon, without a shade,
Slope behind slope, up to the peak, lies bare;
The peak, round which the white clouds play.

    In such a glen, on such a day,
    On Pelion, on the grassy ground,
    Chiron, the aged Centaur, lay,
    The young Achilles standing by.
    The Centaur taught him to explore
    The mountains; where the glens are dry
    And the tired Centaurs come to rest,
    And where the soaking springs abound

And the straight ashes grow for spears,
And where the hill-goats come to feed
And the sea-eagles build their nest.
He show'd him Phthia far away,
And said : O boy, I taught this lore
To Peleus, in long distant years !
He told him of the Gods, the stars,
The tides ;—and then of mortal wars,
And of the life which heroes lead
Before they reach the Elysian place
And rest in the immortal mead ;
And all the wisdom of his race.

The music below ceases, and EMPEDOCLES *speaks,
accompanying himself in a solemn manner on
his harp.*

The out-spread world to span
A cord the Gods first slung,
And then the soul of man
There, like a mirror, hung,
And bade the winds through space impel the gusty
toy.

Hither and thither spins
The wind-borne, mirroring soul;
A thousand glimpses wins,
And never sees a whole;
Looks once, and drives elsewhere, and leaves its last
employ.

The Gods laugh in their sleeve
To watch man doubt and fear,
Who knows not what to believe
Since he sees nothing clear,
And dares stamp nothing false where he finds nothing
sure.

Is this, Pausanias, so?
And can our souls not strive,
But with the winds must go,
And hurry where they drive?
Is Fate indeed so strong, man's strength indeed so poor?

I will not judge! that man,
Howbeit, I judge as lost,
Whose mind allows a plan
Which would degrade it most;
And he treats doubt the best who tries to see least ill.

[DRAM. & LYR.]   C

Be not, then, fear's blind slave!
Thou art my friend; to thee,
All knowledge that I have,
All skill I wield, are free!
Ask not the latest news of the last miracle,

Ask not what days and nights
In trance Pantheia lay,
But ask how thou such sights
May'st see without dismay;
Ask what most helps when known, thou son of
    Anchitus!

What? hate, and awe, and shame
Fill thee to see our world;
Thou feelest thy soul's frame
Shaken and rudely hurl'd?
What? life and time go hard with thee too, as with us;

Thy citizens, 'tis said,
Envy thee and oppress,
Thy goodness no men aid,
All strive to make it less;
Tyranny, pride, and lust fill Sicily's abodes;

Heaven is with earth at strife,
Signs make thy soul afraid,
The dead return to life,
Rivers are dried, winds stay'd;
Scarce can one think in calm, so threatening are the
      Gods;

And we feel, day and night,
The burden of ourselves!—
Well, then, the wiser wight
In his own bosom delves,
And asks what ails him so, and gets what cure he can.

The sophist sneers: Fool, take
Thy pleasure, right or wrong!
The pious wail: Forsake
A world these sophists throng!
Be neither saint nor sophist-led, but be a man.

These hundred doctors try
To preach thee to their school.
We have the truth! they cry;
And yet their oracle,
Trumpet it as they will, is but the same as thine.

Once read thy own breast right,
And thou hast done with fears!
Man gets no other light,
Search he a thousand years.
Sink in thyself! there ask what ails thee, at that shrine!

What makes thee struggle and rave?
Why are men ill at ease? —
'Tis that the lot they have
Fails their own will to please;
For man would make no murmuring, were his will
        obey'd.

And why is it, that still
Man with his lot thus fights?—
'Tis that he makes this *will*
The measure of his *rights*,
And believes Nature outraged if his will's gainsaid.

Couldst thou, Pausanias, learn
How deep a fault is this!
Couldst thou but once discern
Thou hast no *right* to bliss,
No title from the Gods to welfare and repose;

Then thou wouldst look less mazed
Whene'er of bliss debarr'd,
Nor think the Gods were crazed
When thy own lot went hard.
But we are all the same—the fools of our own woes!

For, from the first faint morn
Of life, the thirst for bliss
Deep in man's heart is born!
And, sceptic as he is,
He fails not to judge clear if this be quench'd or no.

Nor is that thirst to blame!
Man errs not that he deems
His welfare his true aim;
He errs because he dreams
The world does but exist that welfare to bestow.

We mortals are no kings
For each of whom to sway
A new-made world up-springs
Meant merely for his play;
No, we are strangers here; the world is from of old.

In vain our pent wills fret,
And would the world subdue.
Limits we did not set
Condition all we do;
Born into life we are, and life must be our mould!

Born into life!—man grows
Forth from his parents' stem,
And blends their bloods, as those
Of theirs are blent in them;
So each new man strikes root into a far fore-time.

Born into life!—we bring
A bias with us here,
And, when here, each new thing
Affects us we come near;
To tunes we did not call our being must keep chime.

Born into life!—in vain,
Opinions, those or these,
Unalter'd to retain
The obstinate mind decrees;
Experience, like a sea, soaks all-effacing in!

Born into life!—who lists
May what is false hold dear,
And for himself make mists
Through which to see less clear;
The world is what it is, for all our dust and din.

Born into life!—'tis we,
And not the world, are new;
Our cry for bliss, our plea,
Others have urged it too—
Our wants have all been felt, our errors made before.

No eye could be too sound
To observe a world so vast,
No patience too profound
To sort what's here amass'd;
How man may here best live no care too great to
     explore.

But we—as some rude guest
Would change, where'er he roam,
The manners there profess'd
To those he brings from home—
We mark not the world's course, but would have *it*
     take *ours*.

The world's course proves the terms
On which man wins content;
Reason the proof confirms;—
We spurn it, and invent
A false course for the world, and for ourselves, false
     powers.

Riches we wish to get,
Yet remain spendthrifts still;
We would have health, and yet
Still use our bodies ill;
Bafflers of our own prayers, from youth to life's last
     scenes!

We would have inward peace,
Yet will not look within;
We would have misery cease,
Yet will not cease from sin;
We want all pleasant ends, but will use no harsh means;

We do not what we ought,
What we ought not, we do,
And lean upon the thought
That chance will bring us through;
But our own acts, for good or ill, are mightier powers!

Yet, even when man forsakes
All sin—is just, is pure,
Abandons all which makes
His welfare insecure—
Other existences there are, that clash with ours.

Like us, the lightning-fires
Love to have scope and play;
The stream, like us, desires
An unimpeded way;
Like us, the Libyan wind delights to roam at large.

Streams will not curb their pride
The just man not to entomb,
Nor lightnings go aside
To give his virtues room;
Nor is that wind less rough which blows a good man's
      barge.

Nature, with equal mind,
Sees all her sons at play;
Sees man control the wind,
The wind sweep man away!
Allows the proudly-riding and the founder'd bark.

And, lastly, though of ours
No weakness spoil our lot,
Though the non-human powers
Of Nature harm us not,
The ill deeds of other men make often *our* life dark.

What were the wise man's plan?—
Through this sharp, toil-set life,
To fight as best he can,
And win what's won by strife!
But we an easier way to cheat our pains have found.

Scratch'd by a fall, with moans
As children of weak age
Lend life to the dumb stones
Whereon to vent their rage,
And bend their little fists, and rate the senseless
    ground;

So, loath to suffer mute,
We, peopling the void air,
Make Gods to whom to impute
The ills we ought to bear;
With God and Fate to rail at, suffering easily.

Yet grant—as sense long miss'd
Things that are now perceived,
And much may still exist
Which is not yet believed—
Grant that the world were full of Gods we cannot see!

All things the world which fill
Of but one stuff are spun,
That we who rail are still,
With what we rail at, one;
One with the o'er-labour'd Power that through the
　　　breadth and length

Of earth, and air, and sea,
In men, and plants, and stones,
Hath toil perpetually,
And travails, strives, and moans;
Fain would do all things well, but sometimes fails in
　　　strength!

And patiently exact
This universal God
Alike to any act
Proceeds at any nod,
And quietly declaims the cursings of himself.

This is not what man hates,
Yet he can curse but this!
Harsh Gods and hostile Fates
Are dreams! this only *is;*
Is everywhere; sustains the wise, the foolish elf.

Nor only, in the intent
To attach blame elsewhere,
Do we at will invent
Stern Powers who make their care
To embitter human life, malignant Deities;

But, next, we would reverse
The scheme ourselves have spun,
And what we made to curse
We now would lean upon,
And feign kind Gods who perfect what man vainly
    tries.

Look, the world tempts our eye,
And we would know it all!
We map the starry sky,
We mine this earthen ball,
We measure the sea-tides, we number the sea-sands;

We scrutinise the dates
Of long-past human things,
The bounds of effaced states,
The lines of deceased kings;
We search out dead men's words, and works of dead
    men's hands;

We shut our eyes, and muse
How our own minds are made,
What springs of thought they use,
How righten'd, how betray'd—
And spend our wit to name what most employ unnamed.

But still, as we proceed,
The mass swells more and more
Of volumes yet to read,
Of secrets yet to explore!
Our hair grows grey, our eyes are dimm'd, our heat
    is tamed.

We rest our faculties,
And thus address the Gods:
'True science if there is,
It stays in your abodes!
Man's measures cannot mete the immeasurable All.

'You only can take in
The world's immense design;
Our desperate search was sin,
Which henceforth we resign,
Sure only that *your* mind sees all things which
　　befal!'

Fools! that in man's brief term
He cannot all things view,
Affords no ground to affirm
That there are Gods who do!
Nor does being weary prove that he has where to rest!

Again: Our youthful blood
Claims rapture as its right;
The world, a rolling flood
Of newness and delight,
Draws in the enamour'd gazer to its shining breast;

Pleasure to our hot grasp
Gives flowers after flowers,
With passionate warmth we clasp
Hand after hand in ours;
Nor do we soon perceive how fast our youth is spent.

At once our eyes grow clear!
We see in blank dismay
Year posting after year,
Sense after sense decay;
Our shivering heart is mined by secret discontent!

Yet still, in spite of truth,
In spite of hopes entomb'd,
That longing of our youth
Burns ever unconsumed,
Still hungrier for delight as delights grow more rare.

We pause; we hush our heart,
And then address the Gods:
'The world hath fail'd to impart
The joy our youth forebodes,
Fail'd to fill up the void which in our breasts we
    bear!

'Changeful till now, we still
Look'd on to something new;
Let us, with changeless will,
Henceforth look on to you,
To find with you the joy we in vain *here* require!'

Fools! that so often here
Happiness mock'd our prayer,
I think, might make us fear
A like event elsewhere!
Make us, not fly to dreams, but moderate desire!

And yet, for those who know
Themselves, who wisely take
Their way through life, and bow
To what they cannot break,
Why should I say that life need yield but *moderate*
    bliss?

Shall we, with temper spoil'd,
Health sapp'd by living ill,
And judgment all embroil'd
By sadness and self-will,
Shall *we* judge what for man is not true bliss or is?

Is it so small a thing
To have enjoy'd the sun,
To have lived light in the spring,
To have loved, to have thought, to have done;
To have advanced true friends, and beat down baffling
    foes;

That we must feign a bliss
Of doubtful future date,
And, while we dream on this,
Lose all our present state,
And relegate to worlds yet distant our repose?

Not much, I know, you prize
What pleasures may be had,
Who look on life with eyes
Estranged, like mine, and sad!
And yet the village-churl feels the truth more than you,

Who 's loath to leave this life
Which to him little yields,
His hard-task'd sunburnt wife,
His often-labour'd fields,
The boors with whom he talk'd, the country-spots he
　　knew.

But thou, because thou hear'st
Men scoff at Heaven and Fate,
Because the Gods thou fear'st
Fail to make blest thy state,
Tremblest, and wilt not dare to trust the joys there are!

I say: Fear not! Life still
Leaves human effort scope.
But, since life teems with ill,
Nurse no extravagant hope;
Because thou must not dream, thou need'st not then
    despair!   .

*A long pause. At the end of it the notes of a harp
   below are again heard, and* CALLICLES *sings :—*

Far, far from here,
The Adriatic breaks in a warm bay
Among the green Illyrian hills! and there
The sunshine in the happy glens is fair,
And by the sea, and in the brakes.
The grass is cool, the sea-side air
Buoyant and fresh, the mountain-flowers
As virginal and sweet as ours.
And there, they say, two bright and aged snakes,
Who once were Cadmus and Harmonia,
Bask in the glens or on the warm sea-shore,
In breathless quiet, after all their ills;
Nor do they see their country, nor the place
Where the Sphinx lived among the frowning hills,

Nor the unhappy palace of their race,
Nor Thebes, nor the Ismenus, any more.

There those two live, far in the Illyrian brakes!
They had stay'd long enough to see,
In Thebes, the billow of calamity
Over their own dear children roll'd,
Curse upon curse, pang upon pang,
For years, they sitting helpless in their home,
A grey old man and woman; yet of old
The Gods had to their marriage come,
And at the banquet all the Muses sang.

Therefore they did not end their days
In sight of blood; but were rapt, far away,
To where the west-wind plays,
And murmurs of the Adriatic come
To those untrodden mountain-lawns; and there
Placed safely in changed forms, the pair
Wholly forget their first sad life, and home,
And all that Theban woe, and stray
For ever through the glens, placid and dumb.

Empedocles.

That was my harp-player again!—where is he?
Down by the stream?

Pausanias.

Yes, Master, in the wood.

Empedocles.

He ever loved the Theban story well!
But the day wears. Go now, Pausanias,
For I must be alone! Leave me one mule;
Take down with thee the rest to Catana.
And for young Callicles, thank him from me!
Tell him I never fail'd to love his lyre;
But he must follow me no more to-night.

Pausanias.

Thou wilt return to-morrow to the city?

Empedocles.

Either to-morrow or some other day,
In the sure revolutions of the world,
Good friend, I shall revisit Catana!
I have seen many cities in my time

Till my eyes ache with the long spectacle,
And I shall doubtless see them all again;
Thou know'st me for a wanderer from of old.
Meanwhile, stay me not now.   Farewell, Pausanias !

He departs on his way up the mountain.

Pausanias (alone).

I dare not urge him further; he must go.
But he is strangely wrought !—I will speed back
And bring Peisianax to him from the city;
His counsel could once soothe him.   But, Apollo !
How his brow lighten'd as the music rose !
Callicles must wait here, and play to him;
I saw him through the chestnuts far below,
Just since, down at the stream.—Ho ! Callicles !

He descends, calling.

ACT II.

Evening.   The Summit of Etna.

EMPEDOCLES.

                    Alone !—
On this charr'd, blacken'd, melancholy waste,
Crown'd by the awful peak, Etna's great mouth,
Round which the sullen vapour rolls—alone !
Pausanias is far hence, and that is well,
For I must henceforth speak no more with man.
He has his lesson too, and that debt's paid;
And the good, learned, friendly, quiet man,
May bravelier front his life, and in himself
Find henceforth energy and heart ! but I,
The weary man, the banish'd citizen—
Whose banishment is not his greatest ill,
Whose weariness no energy can reach,
And for whose hurt courage is not the cure—
What should I do with life and living more?

No, thou art come too late, Empedocles!
And the world hath the day, and must break thee,
Not thou the world! With men thou canst not live,
Their thoughts, their ways, their wishes, are not thine;
And being lonely thou art miserable,
For something has impair'd thy spirit's strength,
And dried its self-sufficing fount of joy.
Thou canst not live with men nor with thyself—
Oh sage! oh sage!—Take then the one way left;
And turn thee to the elements, thy friends,
Thy well-tried friends, thy willing ministers,
And say: Ye servants, hear Empedocles,
Who asks this final service at your hands!
Before the sophist-brood hath overlaid
The last spark of man's consciousness with words—
Ere quite the being of man, ere quite the world
Be disarray'd of their divinity—
Before the soul lose all her solemn joys,
And awe be dead, and hope impossible,
And the soul's deep eternal night come on—
Receive me, hide me, quench me, take me home!

He advances to the edge of the crater. Smoke
and fire break forth with a loud noise, and
CALLICLES *is heard below singing :— .*

The lyre's voice is lovely everywhere !
In the court of Gods, in the city of men,
And in the lonely rock-strewn mountain-glen,
In the still mountain-air.

Only to Typho it sounds hatefully !
To Typho only, the rebel o'erthrown,
Through whose heart Etna drives her roots of stone,
To imbed them in the sea.

Wherefore dost thou groan so loud ?
Wherefore do thy nostrils flash,
Through the dark night, suddenly,
Typho, such red jets of flame ?—
Is thy tortured heart still proud ?
Is thy fire-scathed arm still rash ?
Still alert thy stone-crush'd frame ?
Doth thy fierce soul still deplore
The ancient rout by the Cilician hills,
And that curst treachery on the Mount of Gore ?
Do thy bloodshot eyes still flee

The fight which crown'd thine ills,
Thy last defeat in this Sicilian sea?
Hast thou sworn, in thy sad lair,
Where   erst   the   strong   sea-currents   suck'd   thee
     down,
Never to cease to writhe, and try to sleep,
Letting the sea-stream wander through thy hair?
That thy groans, like thunder deep,
Begin to roll, and almost drown
The sweet notes, whose lulling spell
Gods and the race of mortals love so well,
When through thy caves thou hearest music swell?

But an awful pleasure bland
Spreading o'er the Thunderer's face,
When the sound climbs near his seat,
The Olympian council sees!
As he lets his lax right hand,
Which the lightnings doth embrace,
Sink upon his mighty knees.
And the eagle, at the beck
Of the appeasing gracious harmony,
Droops all his sheeny, brown, deep-feather'd neck,
Nestling nearer to Jove's feet;

While o'er his sovereign eye
The curtains of the blue films slowly meet.
And the white Olympus-peaks
Rosily brighten, and the soothed Gods smile
At one another from their golden chairs,
And no one round the charmed circle speaks.
Only the loved Hebe bears
The cup about, whose draughts beguile
Pain and care, with a dark store
Of fresh-pull'd violets wreathed and nodding o'er;
And her flush'd feet glow on the marble floor.

Empedocles.

He fables, yet speaks truth!
The brave impetuous heart yields everywhere
To the subtle, contriving head!
Great qualities are trodden down;
And littleness united
Is become invincible!

These rumblings are not Typho's groans, I know!
These angry smoke-bursts
Are not the passionate breath
Of the mountain-crush'd, tortured, intractable Titan
      king!

But over all the world
What suffering is there not seen
Of plainness oppress'd by cunning,
As the well-counsell'd Zeus oppress'd
That self-helping son of earth!
What anguish of greatness,
Rail'd and hunted from the world,
Because its simplicity rebukes
This envious, miserable age!

I am weary of it!—
Lie there, ye ensigns
Of my unloved preëminence
In an age like this!
Among a people of children,
Who throng'd me in their cities,
Who worshipp'd me in their houses,
And ask'd, not wisdom,
But drugs to charm with,
But spells to mutter—
All the fool's-armoury of magic!—Lie there,
My golden circlet!
My purple robe!

Callicles (from below).

As the sky-brightening south-wind clears the day,
And makes the mass'd clouds roll,
The music of the lyre blows away
The clouds that wrap the soul.

Oh that Fate had let me see
That triumph of the sweet persuasive lyre,
That famous, final victory
When jealous Pan with Marsyas did conspire !

When, from far Parnassus' side,
Young Apollo, all the pride
Of the Phrygian flutes to tame,
To the Phrygian highlands came !
Where the long green reed-beds sway
In the rippled waters grey
Of that solitary lake
Where Mæander's springs are born ;
Where the ridged pine-wooded roots
Of Messogis westward break,
Mounting westward, high and higher.
There was held the famous strife !

There the Phrygian brought his flutes,
And Apollo brought his lyre!
And, when now the westering sun
Touch'd the hills, the strife was done,
And the attentive Muses said:
'Marsyas! thou art vanquished.'
Then Apollo's minister
Hang'd upon a branching fir
Marsyas, that unhappy Faun,
And began to whet his knife.
But the Mænads, who were there,
Left their friend, and with robes flowing
In the wind, and loose dark hair
O'er their polish'd bosoms blowing,
Each her ribbon'd tambourine
Flinging on the mountain-sod,
With a lovely frighten'd mien
Came about the youthful God.
But he turn'd his beauteous face
Haughtily another way,
From the grassy sun-warm'd place
Where in proud repose he lay,
With one arm over his head,
Watching how the whetting sped.

But aloof, on the lake-strand,
Did the young Olympus stand,
Weeping at his master's end;
For the Faun had been his friend.
For he taught him how to sing,
And he taught him flute-playing.
Many a morning had they gone
To the glimmering mountain-lakes,
And had torn up by the roots
The tall crested water-reeds
With long plumes, and soft brown seeds,
And had carved them into flutes,
Sitting on a tabled stone
Where the shoreward ripple breaks.
And he taught him how to please
The red-snooded Phrygian girls,
Whom the summer evening sees
Flashing in the dance's whirls
Underneath the starlit trees
In the mountain-villages.
Therefore now Olympus stands,
At his master's piteous cries
Pressing fast with both his hands
His white garment to his eyes,

Not to see Apollo's scorn;—
Ah, poor Faun, poor Faun! ah, poor Faun!

Empedocles.

And lie thou there,
My laurel bough!—
Scornful Apollo's ensign, lie thou there!
Though thou hast been my shade in the world's heat—
Though I have loved thee, lived in honouring thee—
Yet lie thou there,
My laurel bough!

I am weary of thee!
I am weary of the solitude
Where he who bears thee must abide!
Of the rocks of Parnassus,
Of the gorge of Delphi,
Of the moonlit peaks, and the caves.
Thou guardest them, Apollo!
Over the grave of the slain Pytho,
Though young, intolerably severe!
Thou keepest aloof the profane,
But the solitude oppresses thy votary!
The jars of men reach him not in thy valley—

But can life reach him?
Thou fencest him from the multitude—
Who will fence him from himself?
He hears nothing but the cry of the torrents,
And the beating of his own heart.
The air is thin, the veins swell—
The temples tighten and throb there!
Air! air!

Take thy bough! set me free from my solitude!
I have been enough alone!

Where shall thy votary fly then? back to men?—
But they will gladly welcome him once more,
And help him to unbend his too tense thought,
And rid him of the presence of himself,
And keep their friendly chatter at his ear,
And haunt him, till the absence from himself,
That other torment, grow unbearable;
And he will fly to solitude again,
And he will find its air too keen for him,
And so change back; and many thousand times
Be miserably bandied to and fro
Like a sea-wave, betwixt the world and thee,

Thou young, implacable God! and only death
Shall cut his oscillations short, and so
Bring him to poise.   There is no other way.

And yet what days were those, Parmenides!
When we were young, when we could number friends
In all the Italian cities like ourselves,
When with elated hearts we join'd your train,
Ye Sun-born Virgins! on the road of truth[2].
Then we could still enjoy, then neither thought
Nor outward things were closed and dead to us,
But we received the shock of mighty thoughts
On simple minds with a pure natural joy;
And if the sacred load oppress'd our brain,
We had the power to feel the pressure eased,
The brow unbound, the thoughts flow free again,
In the delightful commerce of the world.
We had not lost our balance then, nor grown
Thought's slaves, and dead to every natural joy!
The smallest thing could give us pleasure then!
The sports of the country people,
A flute note from the woods,
Sunset over the sea!
Seed-time and harvest,

[DRAM. & LYR.]   E

The reapers in the corn,
The vinedresser in his vineyard,
The village-girl at her wheel!

Fulness of life and power of feeling, ye
Are for the happy, for the souls at ease,
Who dwell on a firm basis of content!—
But he, who has outlived his prosperous days,
But he, whose youth fell on a different world
From that on which his exiled age is thrown,
Whose mind was fed on other food, was train'd
By other rules than are in vogue to-day,
Whose habit of thought is fix'd, who will not
    change,
But in a world he loves not must subsist
In ceaseless opposition, be the guard
Of his own breast, fetter'd to what he guards,
That the world win no mastery over him;
Who has no friend, no fellow left, not one;
Who has no minute's breathing space allow'd
To nurse his dwindling faculty of joy—
Joy and the outward world must die to him,
As they are dead to me!

A long pause, during which EMPEDOCLES *remains motionless, plunged in thought. The night deepens. He moves forward and gazes round him, and proceeds :—*

And you, ye stars,
Who slowly begin to marshal,
As of old, in the fields of Heaven,
Your distant, melancholy lines!
Have *you*, too, survived yourselves?
Are *you*, too, what I fear to become?
You, too, once lived!
You too moved joyfully,
Among august companions,
In an older world, peopled by Gods,
In a mightier order,
The radiant, rejoicing, intelligent Sons of Heaven!
But now, you kindle
Your lonely, cold-shining lights,
Unwilling lingerers
In the heavenly wilderness,
For a younger, ignoble world;
And renew, by necessity,
Night after night your courses,
In echoing unnear'd silence,

Above a race you know not!
Uncaring and undelighted,
Without friend and without home;
Weary like us, though not
Weary with our weariness.

No, no, ye stars! there is no death with you,
No languor, no decay! Languor and death,
They are with me, not you! ye are alive!
Ye and the pure dark ether where ye ride
Brilliant above me! And thou, fiery world,
That sapp'st the vitals of this terrible mount
Upon whose charr'd and quaking crust I stand—
Thou, too, brimmest with life!—the sea of cloud
That heaves its white and billowy vapours up
To moat this isle of ashes from the world,
Lives!—and that other fainter sea, far down,
O'er whose lit floor a road of moonbeams leads
To Etna's Liparëan sister-fires
And the long dusky line of Italy—
That mild and luminous floor of waters lives,
With held-in joy swelling its heart!—I only,
Whose spring of hope is dried, whose spirit has
    fail'd—

I, who have not, like these, in solitude
Maintain'd courage and force, and in myself
Nursed an immortal vigour—I alone
Am dead to life and joy! therefore I read
In all things my own deadness.

A long silence.   He continues :—

Oh that I could glow like this mountain!
Oh that my heart bounded with the swell of the
    sea!
Oh that my soul were full of light as the stars!
Oh that it brooded over the world like the air!

But no, this heart will glow no more! thou art
A living man no more, Empedocles!
Nothing but a devouring flame of thought—
But a naked, eternally restless mind!

After a pause :—

To the elements it came from
Everything will return.
Our bodies to earth,
Our blood to water,
Heat to fire,
Breath to air.

They were well born, they will be well entomb'd!
But mind? . . .

And we might gladly share the fruitful stir
Down in our mother earth's miraculous womb!
Well would it be
With what roll'd of us in the stormy main!
We might have joy, blent with the all-bathing air,
Or with the nimble radiant life of fire!

But mind—but thought—
If these have been the master part of us—
Where will *they* find their parent element?
What will receive *them*, who will call *them* home?
But we shall still be in them, and they in us,
And we shall be the strangers of the world,
And they will be our lords, as they are now;
And keep us prisoners of our consciousness,
And never let us clasp and feel the All
But through their forms, and modes, and stifling veils.
And we shall be unsatisfied as now;
And we shall feel the agony of thirst,
The ineffable longing for the life of life
Baffled for ever; and still thought and mind

Will hurry us with them on their homeless march,
Over the unallied unopening earth,
Over the unrecognising sea; while air
Will blow us fiercely back to sea and earth,
And fire repel us from its living waves.
And then we shall unwillingly return
Back to this meadow of calamity,
This uncongenial place, this human life!
And in our individual human state
Go through the sad probation all again,
To see if we will poise our life at last,
To see if we will now at last be true
To our own only true, deep-buried selves,
Being one with which we are one with the whole
    world;
Or whether we will once more fall away
Into some bondage of the flesh or mind,
Some slough of sense, or some fantastic maze
Forged by the imperious lonely thinking-power.
And each succeeding age in which we are born
Will have more peril for us than the last;
Will goad our senses with a sharper spur,
Will fret our minds to an intenser play,
Will make ourselves harder to be discern'd.

And we shall struggle awhile, gasp and rebel;
And we shall fly for refuge to past times,
Their soul of unworn youth, their breath of greatness;
And the reality will pluck us back,
Knead us in its hot hand, and change our nature!
And we shall feel our powers of effort flag,
And rally them for one last fight, and fail;
And we shall sink in the impossible strife,
And be astray for ever!

      Slave of sense
I have in no wise been! but slave of thought?—
And who can say: I have been always free,
Lived ever in the light of my own soul?—
I cannot! I have lived in wrath and gloom,
Fierce, disputatious, ever at war with man,
Far from my own soul, far from warmth and light.
But I have not grown easy in these bonds—
But I have not denied what bonds these were!
Yea, I take myself to witness,
That I have loved no darkness,
Sophisticated no truth,
Nursed no delusion,
Allow'd no fear!

And therefore, O ye elements, I know—
Ye know it too—it hath been granted me
Not to die wholly, not to be all enslaved!
I feel it in this hour! The numbing cloud
Mounts off my soul; I feel it, I breathe free!

Is it but for a moment?—
Ah! boil up, ye vapours!
Leap and roar, thou sea of fire!
My soul glows to meet you.
Ere it flag, ere the mists
Of despondency and gloom
Rush over it again,
Receive me! save me!　　*He plunges into the crater.*

Callicles (from below).

Through the black, rushing smoke-bursts,
Thick breaks the red flame;
All Etna heaves fiercely
Her forest-clothed frame.

Not here, O Apollo!
Are haunts meet for thee.
But, where Helicon breaks down
In cliff to the sea,

Where the moon-silver'd inlets
Send far their light voice
Up the still vale of Thisbe,
O speed, and rejoice !

On the sward at the cliff-top
Lie strewn the white flocks;
On the cliff-side the pigeons
Roost deep in the rocks.

In the moonlight the shepherds,
Soft lull'd by the rills,
Lie wrapt in their blankets,
Asleep on the hills.

—What forms are these coming
So white through the gloom?
What garments out-glistening
The gold-flower'd broom?

What sweet-breathing presence
Out-perfumes the thyme?
What voices enrapture
The night's balmy prime?—

'Tis Apollo comes leading
His choir, the Nine.
—The leader is fairest,
But all are divine.

They are lost in the hollows!
They stream up again!
What seeks on this mountain
The glorified train?—

They bathe on this mountain,
In the spring by their road;
Then on to Olympus,
Their endless abode!

—Whose praise do they mention?
Of what is it told?—
What will be for ever;
What was from of old.

First hymn they the Father
Of all things;—and then,
The rest of immortals,
The action of men.

The day in his hotness,
The strife with the palm;
The night in her silence,
The stars in their calm.

FRAGMENT OF AN 'ANTIGONE.'

The Chorus.

WELL hath he done who hath seized happiness!
    For little do the all-containing Hours,
      Though opulent, freely give.
      Who, weighing that life well
      Fortune presents unpray'd,
Declines her ministry, and carves his own;
      And, justice not infringed,
Makes his own welfare his unswerved-from law!

He does well too, who keeps that clue the mild
Birth-Goddess and the austere Fates first gave!
      For from the day when these
      Bring him, a weeping child,
      First to the light, and mark
A country for him, kinsfolk, and a home,
      Unguided he remains,
Till the Fates come again, alone, with death.

In little companies,
And, our own place once left,
Ignorant where to stand, or whom to avoid,
By city and household group'd, we live! and many
        shocks
    Our order heaven-ordain'd
    Must every day endure—
Voyages, exiles, hates, dissensions, wars!
    Besides what waste *he* makes,
    The all-hated, order-breaking,
    Without friend, city, or home,
    Death, who dissevers all.

    Him then I praise, who dares
    To self-selected good
Prefer obedience to the primal law,
Which consecrates the ties of blood; for these, indeed,
    Are to the Gods a care!
    That touches but himself!
For every day man may be link'd and loosed
    With strangers; but the bond
    Original, deep-inwound,
    Of blood, can he not bind,
    Nor, if Fate binds, not bear.

But hush! Hæmon, whom Antigone,
Robbing herself of life in burying,
Against Creon's law, Polynices,
Robs of a loved bride—pale, imploring,
    Waiting her passage,
Forth from the palace hitherward comes!

Hæmon.

No, no, old men, Creon I curse not!
    I weep, Thebans,
   One than Creon crueller far.
For he, he, at least, by slaying her,
August laws doth mightily vindicate;
But thou, too-bold, headstrong, pitiless!
Ah me!—honourest more than thy lover,
    O Antigone!
A dead, ignorant, thankless corpse.

The Chorus.

   Nor was the love untrue
   Which the Dawn-Goddess bore
   To that fair youth she erst,
   Leaving the salt sea-beds
And coming flush'd over the stormy frith

Of loud Euripus, saw—
Saw and snatch'd, wild with love,
From the pine-dotted spurs
Of Parnes, where thy waves,
Asopus! gleam rock-hemm'd—
The Hunter of the Tanagræan Field.[8]

But him, in his sweet prime,
By severance immature,
By Artemis' soft shafts,
She, though a Goddess born,
Saw in the rocky isle of Delos die.
Such end o'ertook that love!
For she desired to make
Immortal mortal man,
And blend his happy life,
Far from the Gods, with hers;
To him postponing an eternal law.

Hæmon.

But, like me, she, wroth, complaining,
Succumb'd to the envy of unkind Gods;
And, her beautiful arms unclasping,
Her fair youth unwillingly gave.

The Chorus.

Nor, though enthroned too high
To fear assault of envious Gods,
His beloved Argive seer would Zeus retain
From his appointed end
In this our Thebes; but when

His flying steeds came near
To cross the steep Ismenian glen,
The broad earth open'd and whelm'd them and him;
And through the void air sang
At large his enemy's spear.

And fain would Zeus have saved his tired son
Beholding him where the Two Pillars stand
O'er the sun-redden'd western straits,[4]
Or at his work in that dim lower world;
Fain would he have recall'd
The fraudulent oath which bound
To a much feebler wight the heroic man;

But he preferr'd Fate to his strong desire.
Nor did there need less than the burning pile

[DRAM. & LYR.]   F

Under the towering Trachis crags,
And the Spercheios vale, shaken with groans,
And the roused Maliac gulph,
And scared Œtæan snows,
To achieve his son's deliverance, O my child!

FRAGMENT OF CHORUS OF A
DEJANEIRA.

O FRIVOLOUS mind of man,
  Light ignorance, and hurrying, unsure thoughts,
Though man bewails you not,
How *I* bewail you!

Little in your prosperity
Do you seek counsel of the Gods.
Proud, ignorant, self-adored, you live alone.
In profound silence stern
Among their savage gorges and cold springs
Unvisited remain
The great oracular shrines.

Thither in your adversity
Do you betake yourselves for light,
But strangely misinterpret all you hear.
For you will not put on

New hearts with the enquirer's holy robe,
And purged, considerate minds.

And him on whom, at the end
Of toil and dolour untold,
The Gods have said that repose
At last shall descend undisturb'd,
Him you expect to behold
In an easy old age, in a happy home;
No end but this you praise.

But him, on whom, in the prime
Of life, with vigour undimm'd,
With unspent mind, and a soul
Unworn, undebased, undecay'd,
Mournfully grating, the gates
Of the city of death have for ever closed—
Him, I count *him*, well-starr'd.

PHILOMELA.

HARK! ah, the nightingale!
   The tawny-throated!
Hark! from that moonlit cedar what a burst!
What triumph! hark—what pain!

O wanderer from a Grecian shore,
Still, after many years, in distant lands,
Still nourishing in thy bewilder'd brain
That wild, unquench'd, deep-sunken, old-world pain—
Say, will it never heal?
And can this fragrant lawn
With its cool trees, and night,
And the sweet, tranquil Thames,
And moonshine, and the dew,
To thy rack'd heart and brain
Afford no balm?

Dost thou to-night behold,
Here, through the moonlight on this English grass,
The unfriendly palace in the Thracian wild?

Dost thou again peruse

With hot cheeks and sear'd eyes

The too clear web, and thy dumb sister's shame?

Dost thou once more assay

Thy flight, and feel come over thee,

Poor fugitive, the feathery change

Once more, and once more seem to make resound

With love and hate, triumph and agony,

Lone Daulis, and the high Cephissian vale?

Listen, Eugenia—

How thick the bursts come crowding through the
      leaves!

Again—thou hearest?

Eternal passion!

Eternal pain!

EARLY DEATH AND FAME.

FOR him who must see many years,
   I praise the life which slips away
Out of the light and mutely; which avoids
Fame, and her less fair followers, envy, strife,
Stupid detraction, jealousy, cabal,
Insincere praises; which descends
The quiet mossy track to age.

But, when immature death
Beckons too early the guest
From the half-tried banquet of life,
Young, in the bloom of his days;
Leaves no leisure to press,
Slow and surely, the sweets
Of a tranquil life in the shade—
Fuller for him be the hours!
Give him emotion, though pain!
Let him live, let him feel: *I have lived!*
Heap up his moments with life,
Triple his pulses with fame!

BACCHANALIA;

OR,

THE NEW AGE.

I.

THE evening comes, the field is still.
 The tinkle of the thirsty rill,
Unheard all day, ascends again;
Deserted is the half-mown plain,
Silent the swaths! the ringing wain,
The mower's cry, the dog's alarms,
All housed within the sleeping farms!
The business of the day is done,
The last-left haymaker is gone.
And from the thyme upon the height,
And from the elder-blossom white
And pale dog-roses in the hedge,
And from the mint-plant in the sedge,
In puffs of balm the night-air blows
The perfume which the day forgoes.

And on the pure horizon far,
See, pulsing with the first-born star,
The liquid sky above the hill!
The evening comes, the field is still.

Loitering and leaping,
With saunter, with bounds—
Flickering and circling
In files and in rounds—
Gaily their pine-staff green
Tossing in air,
Loose o'er their shoulders white
Showering their hair—
See! the wild Mænads
Break from the wood,
Youth and Iacchus
Maddening their blood!
See! through the quiet land
Rioting they pass—
Fling the fresh heaps about,
Trample the grass!
Tear from the rifled hedge
Garlands, their prize;

Fill with their sports the field,
Fill with their cries!

Shepherd, what ails thee, then?
Shepherd, why mute?
Forth with thy joyous song!
Forth with thy flute!
Tempts not the revel blithe?
Lure not their cries?
Glow not their shoulders smooth?
Melt not their eyes?
Is not, on cheeks like those,
Lovely the flush?
—*Ah, so the quiet was!*
So was the hush!

II.

The epoch ends, the world is still.
The age has talk'd and work'd its fill—
The famous orators have shone,
The famous poets sung and gone,
The famous men of war have fought,
The famous speculators thought,
The famous players, sculptors, wrought,

The famous painters fill'd their wall,
The famous critics judged it all.
The combatants are parted now,
Uphung the spear, unbent the bow,
The puissant crown'd, the weak laid low!
And in the after-silence sweet,
Now strife is hush'd, our ears doth meet,
Ascending pure, the bell-like fame
Of this or that down-trodden name,
Delicate spirits, push'd away
In the hot press of the noon-day.
And o'er the plain, where the dead age
Did its now silent warfare wage—
O'er that wide plain, now wrapt in gloom,
Where many a splendour finds its tomb,
Many spent fames and fallen nights—
The one or two immortal lights
Rise slowly up into the sky
To shine there everlastingly,
Like stars over the bounding hill.
The epoch ends, the world is still.

Thundering and bursting
In torrents, in waves—

Carolling and shouting
Over tombs, amid graves—
See! on the cumber'd plain
Clearing a stage,
Scattering the past about,
Comes the new age!
Bards make new poems,
Thinkers new schools,
Statesmen new systems,
Critics new rules!
All things begin again;
Life is their prize;
Earth with their deeds they fill,
Fill with their cries!

Poet, what ails thee, then?
Say, why so mute?
Forth with thy praising voice!
Forth with thy flute!
Loiterer! why sittest thou
Sunk in thy dream?
Tempts not the bright new age?
Shines not its stream?
Look, ah, what genius,

Art, science, wit !
Soldiers like Cæsar,
Statesmen like Pitt !
Sculptors like Phidias,
Raphaels in shoals,
Poets like Shakspeare—
Beautiful souls !
See, on their glowing cheeks
Heavenly the flush !
—Ah, so the silence was !
So was the hush !

The world but feels the present's spell,
The poet feels the past as well;
Whatever men have done, might do,
Whatever thought, might think it too.

SWITZERLAND.

1. *A Memory-Picture.*

YOUNG, I said: 'A face is gone
   If too hotly mused upon;
And our best impressions are
Those that do themselves repair.'
Many a face I then let flee,
Ah, is faded utterly!
   Ere the parting hour go by,
   Quick, thy tablets, Memory!

Marguerite says: 'As last year went,
So the coming year 'll be spent!
Some day next year, I shall be,
Entering heedless, kiss'd by thee.'
Ah! I hope—yet, once away,
What may chain us, who can say?
   Ere the parting hour go by,
   Quick, thy tablets, Memory!

Paint that lilac kerchief, bound
Her soft face, her hair around;
Tied under the archest chin
Mockery ever ambush'd in!
Let the fluttering fringes streak
All her pale, sweet-rounded cheek!
  Ere the parting hour go by,
  Quick, thy tablets, Memory!

Paint that figure's pliant grace
As she toward me lean'd her face,
Half refused and half resign'd,
Murmuring: 'Art thou still unkind?'
Many a broken promise then   .
Was new made—to break again.
  Ere the parting hour go by,
  Quick, thy tablets, Memory!

Paint those eyes, so blue, so kind,
Eager tell-tales of her mind!
Paint, with their impetuous stress
Of enquiring tenderness,
Those frank eyes, where deep doth lie
An angelic gravity!

Ere the parting hour go by,
Quick, thy tablets, Memory!

What, my friends, these feeble lines
Shew, you say, my love declines?
To paint ill as I have done,
Proves forgetfulness begun?
Time's gay minions, pleased you see,
Time, your master, governs me;
    Pleased, you mock the fruitless cry:
    'Quick, thy tablets, Memory!'

Ah, too true! Time's current strong
Leaves us firm to nothing long.
Yet, if little stays with man,
Ah, retain we all we can!
If the clear impression dies,
Ah! the dim remembrance prize!
    Ere the parting hour go by,
    Quick, thy tablets, Memory!

2. *Meeting.*

AGAIN I see my bliss at hand!
  The town, the lake are here.
My Marguerite smiles upon the strand
Unalter'd with the year.

I know that graceful figure fair,
That cheek of languid hue;
I know that soft enkerchief'd hair,
And those sweet eyes of blue.

Again I spring to make my choice;
Again in tones of ire
I hear a God's tremendous voice:
'Be counsell'd, and retire!'

Ye guiding Powers who join and part,
What would ye have with me?
Ah, warn some more ambitious heart,
And let the peaceful be!

3. *Parting.*

YE storm-winds of Autumn !
   Who rush by, who shake
The window, and ruffle
The gleam-lighted lake ;
Who cross to the hill-side
Thin-sprinkled with farms,
Where the high woods strip sadly
Their yellowing arms ;—
Ye are bound for the mountains !
Ah, with you let me go
Where your cold distant barrier,
The vast range of snow,
Through the loose clouds lifts dimly
Its white peaks in air—
How deep is their stillness !
Ah ! would I were there !

But on the stairs what voice is this I hear,
Buoyant as morning, and as morning clear ?

Say, has some wet bird-haunted English lawn
Lent it the music of its trees at dawn?
Or was it from some sun-fleck'd mountain-brook
That the sweet voice its upland clearness took?
      Ah! it comes nearer—
      Sweet notes, this way!

    Hark! fast by the window
    The rushing winds go,
    To the ice-cumber'd gorges,
    The vast seas of snow.
    There the torrents drive upward
    Their rock-strangled hum,
    There the avalanche thunders
    The hoarse torrent dumb.
    —I come, O ye mountains!
    Ye torrents, I come!

But who is this, by the half-open'd door,
Whose figure casts a shadow on the floor?
The sweet blue eyes—the soft, ash-colour'd hair—
The cheeks that still their gentle paleness wear—
The lovely lips, with their arch smile that tells
The unconquer'd joy in which her spirit dwells—

Ah! they bend nearer—
Sweet lips, this way!

Hark! the wind rushes past us—
Ah! with that let me go
To the clear waning hill-side
Unspotted by snow,
There to watch, o'er the sunk vale,
The frore mountain wall,
Where the niched snow-bed sprays down
Its powdery fall!
There its dusky blue clusters
The aconite spreads;
There the pines slope, the cloud-strips
Hung soft in their heads!
No life but, at moments,
The mountain-bee's hum.
—I come, O ye mountains!
Ye pine-woods, I come!

Forgive me! forgive me!
　Ah, Marguerite, fain
Would these arms reach to clasp thee!—
　But see! 'tis in vain.

In the void air towards thee
　My strain'd arms are cast;
But a sea rolls between us—
　Our different past!

To the lips, ah! of others,
　Those lips have been prest,
And others, ere I was,
　Were clasp'd to that breast;

Far, far from each other
　Our spirits have grown;
And what heart knows another?
　Ah! who knows his own?

Blow, ye winds! lift me with you!
　I come to the wild.
Fold closely, O Nature!
　Thine arms round thy child.

To thee only God granted
　A heart ever new—
To all always open,
　To all always true.

Ah, calm me! restore me!
And dry up my tears
On thy high mountain platforms,
 Where morn first appears,

Where the white mists, for ever,
 Are spread and upfurl'd;
In the stir of the forces
 Whence issued the world.

4. *A Farewell.*

M^Y horse's feet beside the lake,
   Where sweet the unbroken moonbeams lay,
Sent echoes through the night to wake
Each glistening strand, each heath-fringed bay.

The poplar avenue was pass'd,
And the roof'd bridge that spans the stream.
Up the steep street I hurried fast,
Led by thy taper's starlike beam.

I came ! I saw thee rise !—the blood
Pour'd flushing to thy languid cheek.
Lock'd in each other's arms we stood,
In tears, with hearts too full to speak.

Days flew ;—ah, soon I could discern
A trouble in thine alter'd air !
Thy hand lay languidly in mine,
Thy cheek was grave, thy speech grew rare.

I blame thee not!—this heart, I know,
To be long loved was never framed;
For something in its depths doth glow
Too strange, too restless, too untamed.

And women—things that live and move
Mined by the fever of the soul—
They seek to find in those they love
Stern strength, and promise of control.

They ask not kindness, gentle ways;
These they themselves have tried and known.
They ask a soul which never sways
With the blind gusts that shake their own.

I too have felt the load I bore
In a too strong emotion's sway;
I too have wish'd, no woman more,
This starting, feverish, heart away.

I too have long'd for trenchant force
And will like a dividing spear;
Have praised the keen, unscrupulous course,
Which knows no doubt, which feels no fear.

But in the world I learnt, what there
Thou too wilt surely one day prove,
That will, that energy, though rare,
Are yet far, far less rare than love!

Go then! till time and fate impress
This truth on thee, be mine no more!
They will!—for thou, I feel, no less
Than I, wast destined to this lore.

We school our manners, act our parts—
But He, who sees us through and through,
Knows that the bent of both our hearts
Was to be gentle, tranquil, true.

And though we wear out life, alas!
Distracted as a homeless wind,
In beating where we must not pass,
In seeking what we shall not find;

Yet we shall one day gain, life past,
Clear prospect o'er our being's whole;
Shall see ourselves, and learn at last
Our true affinities of soul.

We shall not then deny a course
To every thought the mass ignore;
We shall not then call hardness force,
Nor lightness wisdom any more.

Then, in the eternal Father's smile,
Our soothed, encouraged souls will dare
To *seem* as free from pride and guile,
As good, as generous, as they *are*.

Then we shall know our friends ! though much
Will have been lost—the help in strife,
The thousand sweet, still joys, of such
As hand in hand face earthly life—

Though these be lost, there will be yet
A sympathy august and pure;
Ennobled by a vast regret,
And by contrition seal'd thrice sure.

And we, whose ways were unlike here,
May then more neighbouring courses ply;
May to each other be brought near
And greet across infinity.

How sweet, unreach'd by earthly jars,
My sister! to behold with thee
The hush among the shining stars,
The calm upon the moonlit sea!

How sweet to feel, on the boon air,
All our unquiet pulses cease!
To feel that nothing can impair
The gentleness, the thirst for peace—

The gentleness too rudely hurl'd
On this wild earth of hate and fear;
The thirst for peace a raving world
Would never let us satiate here.

5. *Absence.*

IN this fair stranger's eyes of grey
  Thine eyes, my love! I see.
I shudder! for the passing day
Had borne me far from thee.

This is the curse of life! that not
A nobler, calmer train
Of wiser thoughts and feelings blot
Our passions from our brain;

But each day brings its petty dust
Our soon-choked souls to fill,
And we forget because we must,
And not because we will.

I struggle towards the light; and ye,
Once-long'd-for storms of love!
If with the light ye cannot be,
I bear that ye remove.

I struggle towards the light—but oh,
While yet the night is chill,
Upon time's barren, stormy flow,
Stay with me, Marguerite, still!

6. *Isolation. To Marguerite.*

WE were apart! yet, day by day,
  I bade my heart more constant be;
I bade it keep the world away,
And grow a home for only thee;
Nor fear'd but thy love likewise grew,
Like mine, each day more tried, more true.

The fault was grave! I might have known,
What far too soon, alas, I learn'd—
The heart can bind itself alone,
And faith is often unreturn'd.
Self-sway'd our feelings ebb and swell!
Thou lov'st no more;—Farewell! Farewell!

Farewell!—and thou, thou lonely heart,
Which never yet without remorse
Even for a moment didst depart
From thy remote and spheréd course

To haunt the place where passions reign—
Back to thy solitude again!

Back! with the conscious thrill of shame
Which Luna felt, that summer night,
Flash through her pure immortal frame,
When she forsook the starry height
To hang over Endymion's sleep
Upon the pine-grown Latmian steep—

Yet she, chaste queen, had never proved
How vain a thing is mortal love,
Wandering in Heaven, far removed;
But thou hast long had place to prove
This truth—to prove, and make thine own:
'Thou hast been, shalt be, art, alone!'

Or, if not quite alone, yet they
Which touch thee are unmating things—
Ocean and clouds and night and day;
Lorn autumns and triumphant springs;
And life, and others' joy and pain,
And love, if love, of happier men.

Of happier men!—for they, at least,
Have dream'd two human hearts might blend
In one, and were through faith released
From isolation without end
Prolong'd; nor knew, although not less
Alone than thou, their loneliness!

7. *To Marguerite. Continued.*

YES! in the sea of life enisled,
  With echoing straits between us thrown,
Dotting the shoreless watery wild,
We mortal millions live *alone.*
The islands feel the enclasping flow,
And then their endless bounds they know.

But when the moon their hollows lights,
And they are swept by balms of spring,
And in their glens, on starry nights,
The nightingales divinely sing;
And lovely notes, from shore to shore,
Across the sounds and channels pour—

Oh! then a longing like despair
Is to their farthest caverns sent;
For surely once, they feel, we were
Parts of a single continent!
Now round us spreads the watery plain—
Oh might our marges meet again!

[DRAM. & LYR.]   H

Who order'd, that their longing's fire
Should be, as soon as kindled, cool'd?
Who renders vain their deep desire?—
A God, a God their severance ruled!
And bade betwixt their shores to be
The unplumb'd, salt, estranging sea.

8. *The Terrace at Berne.*

(COMPOSED TEN YEARS AFTER THE PRECEDING.)

TEN years!—and to my waking eye
   Once more the roofs of Berne appear;
The rocky banks, the terrace high,
The stream!—and do I linger here?

The clouds are on the Oberland,
The Jungfrau snows look faint and far;
But bright are those green fields at hand,
And through those fields comes down the Aar,

And from the blue twin-lakes it comes,
Flows by the town, the church-yard fair;
And 'neath the garden-walk it hums,
The house!—and is my Marguerite there?

Ah, shall I see thee, while a flush
Of startled pleasure floods thy brow,
Quick through the oleanders brush,
And clap thy hands, and cry: *'Tis thou!*

H 2

Or hast thou long since wander'd back,
Daughter of France! to France, thy home;
And flitted down the flowery track
Where feet like thine too lightly come?

Doth riotous laughter now replace
Thy smile, and rouge, with stony glare,
Thy cheek's soft hue, and fluttering lace
The kerchief that enwound thy hair?

Or is it over?—art thou dead?—
Dead!—and no warning shiver ran
Across my heart, to say thy thread
Of life was cut, and closed thy span!

Could from earth's ways that figure slight
Be lost, and I not feel 'twas so?
Of that fresh voice the gay delight
Fail from earth's air and I not know?

Or shall I find thee still, but changed,
But not the Marguerite of thy prime?
With all thy being re-arranged,
Pass'd through the crucible of time;

With spirit vanish'd, beauty waned,
And hardly yet a glance, a tone,
A gesture—anything—retain'd
Of all that was my Marguerite's own?

I will not know!—for wherefore try
To things by mortal course that live
A shadowy durability,
For which they were not meant, to give?

Like driftwood spars which meet and pass
Upon the boundless ocean-plain,
So on the sea of life, alas!
Man nears man, meets, and leaves again.

I knew it when my life was young!
I feel it still, now youth is o'er!
The mists are on the mountains hung,
And Marguerite I shall see no more.

URANIA.

SHE smiles and smiles, and will not sigh,
    While we for hopeless passion die;
Yet she could love, those eyes declare,
Were but men nobler than they are.

Eagerly once her gracious ken
Was turn'd upon the sons of men;
But light the serious visage grew—
She look'd, and smiled, and saw them through!

Our petty souls, our strutting wits,
Our labour'd, puny passion-fits—
Ah, may she scorn them still, till we
Scorn them as bitterly as she!

Yet show her once, ye heavenly Powers,
One of some worthier race than ours!
One for whose sake she once might prove
How deeply she who scorns can love.

His eyes be like the starry lights—
His voice like sounds of summer nights—
In all his lovely mien let pierce
The magic of the universe!

And she to him will reach her hand,
And gazing in his eyes will stand,
And know her friend, and weep for glee,
And cry: *Long, long I've look'd for thee.*

Then will she weep !—with smiles, till then,
Coldly she mocks the sons of men.
Till then her lovely eyes maintain
Their pure, unwavering, deep disdain.

EUPHROSYNE.

I WILL not say that thou wast true,
  Yet let me say that thou wast fair!
And they that lovely face who view,
They should not ask if truth be there.

Truth—what is truth? Two bleeding hearts
Wounded by men, by Fortune tried,
Outwearied with their lonely parts,
Vow to beat henceforth side by side.

The world to them was stern and drear,
Their lot was but to weep and moan;
Ah, let them keep their faith sincere,
For neither could subsist alone!

But souls whom some benignant breath
Has charm'd at birth from gloom and care,
These ask no love, these plight no faith,
For they are happy as they are.

The world to them may homage make,
And garlands for their forehead weave;
And what the world can give, they take—
But they bring more than they receive.

They smile upon the world! their ears
To one demand alone are coy;
They will not give us love and tears—
They bring us light, and warmth, and joy.

On one she smiled, and he was blest!
She smiles elsewhere—we make a din!
But 'twas not love which heaved her breast,
Fair child!—it was the bliss within.

CALAIS SANDS.

A THOUSAND knights have rein'd their steeds
    To watch this line of sand-hills run,
Along the never-silent strait,
To Calais glittering in the sun.

To look toward Ardres' Golden Field
Across this wide aërial plain,
Which glows as if the Middle Age
Were gorgeous upon earth again.

Oh, that to share this famous scene
I saw, upon the open sand,
Thy lovely presence at my side,
Thy shawl, thy look, thy smile, thy hand!

How exquisite thy voice would come,
My darling, on this lonely air!
How sweetly would the fresh sea-breeze
Shake loose some lock of soft brown hair!

But now my glance but once hath roved
O'er Calais and its famous plain;
To England's cliffs my gaze is turn'd,
O'er the blue strait mine eyes I strain.

Thou comest! Yes, the vessel's cloud
Hangs dark upon the rolling sea!—
Oh that yon sea-bird's wings were mine
To win one instant's glimpse of thee!

I must not spring to grasp thy hand,
To woo thy smile, to seek thine eye;
But I may stand far off, and gaze,
And watch thee pass unconscious by,

And spell thy looks, and guess thy thoughts,
Mixt with the idlers on the pier;—
Ah, might I always rest unseen,
So I might have thee always near!

To-morrow hurry through the fields
Of Flanders to the storied Rhine!
To-night those soft-fringed eyes shall close
Beneath one roof, my queen! with mine.

DOVER BEACH.

THE sea is calm to-night,
  The tide is full, the moon lies fair
Upon the straits;—on the French coast, the light
Gleams, and is gone; the cliffs of England stand,
Glimmering and vast, out in the tranquil bay.
Come to the window, sweet is the night air!
Only, from the long line of spray
Where the ebb meets the moon-blanch'd sand,
Listen! you hear the grating roar
Of pebbles which the waves draw back, and fling,
At their return, up the high strand,
Begin, and cease, and then again begin,
With tremulous cadence slow, and bring
The eternal note of sadness in.

Sophocles long ago
Heard it on the Ægæan, and it brought
Into his mind the turbid ebb and flow
Of human misery; we
Find also in the sound a thought,
Hearing it by this distant northern sea.

The Sea of Faith
Was once, too, at the full, and round earth's shore
Lay like the folds of a bright girdle furl'd;
But now I only hear
Its melancholy, long, withdrawing roar,
Retreating to the breath
Of the night-wind down the vast edges drear
And naked shingles of the world.

Ah, love, let us be true
To one another! for the world, which seems
To lie before us like a land of dreams,
So various, so beautiful, so new,
Hath really neither joy, nor love, nor light,
Nor certitude, nor peace, nor help for pain;
And we are here as on a darkling plain
Swept with confused alarms of struggle and fight,
Where ignorant armies clash by night!

THE BURIED LIFE.

LIGHT flows our war of mocking words, and yet,
    Behold, with tears mine eyes are wet!
I feel a nameless sadness o'er me roll.
Yes, yes, we know that we can jest,
We know, we know that we can smile!
But there's a something in this breast
To which thy light words bring no rest,
And thy gay smiles no anodyne;
Give me thy hand, and hush awhile,
And turn those limpid eyes on mine,
And let me read there, love, thy inmost soul!

Alas, is even love too weak
To unlock the heart, and let it speak?
Are even lovers powerless to reveal
To one another what indeed they feel?
I knew the mass of men conceal'd
Their thoughts, for fear that if reveal'd
They would by other men be met
With blank indifference, or with blame reproved;

I knew they lived and moved
Trick'd in disguises, alien to the rest
Of men, and alien to themselves!—and yet
The same heart beats in every human breast.

But we, my love—doth a like spell benumb
Our hearts?—our voices?—must we too be dumb?

Ah! well for us, if even we,
Even for a moment, can get free
Our heart, and have our lips unchain'd;
For that which seals them hath been deep ordain'd!

Fate, which foresaw
How frivolous a baby man would be,
By what distractions he would be possess'd,
How he would pour himself in every strife,
And well-nigh change his own identity;
That it might keep from his capricious play
His genuine self, and force him to obey
Even in his own despite his being's law,
Bade through the deep recesses of our breast
The unregarded river of our life
Pursue with indiscernible flow its way;

And that we should not see
The buried stream, and seem to be
Eddying at large in blind uncertainty,
Though driving on with it eternally.

But often, in the world's most crowded streets,
But often, in the din of strife,
There rises an unspeakable desire
After the knowledge of our buried life,
A thirst to spend our fire and restless force
In tracking out our true, original course;
A longing to inquire
Into the mystery of this heart which beats
So wild, so deep in us,— to know
Whence our thoughts come and where they go.
And many a man in his own breast then delves,
But deep enough, alas, none ever mines!
And we have been on many thousand lines,
And we have shown, on each, spirit and power;
But hardly have we, for one little hour,
Been on our own line, have we been ourselves!
Hardly had skill to utter one of all
The nameless feelings that course through our breast,
But they course on for ever unexpress'd!

And long we try in vain to speak and act
Our hidden self, and what we say and do
Is eloquent, is well—but 'tis not true!
And then we will no more be rack'd
With inward striving, and demand
Of all the thousand nothings of the hour
Their stupefying power;
Ah yes, and they benumb us at our call!
Yet still, from time to time, vague and forlorn,
From the soul's subterranean depth upborne
As from an infinitely distant land,
Come airs, and floating echoes, and convey
A melancholy into all our day.

Only, but this is rare!
When a belovéd hand is laid in ours,
When, jaded with the rush and glare
Of the interminable hours,
Our eyes can in another's eyes read clear,
When our world-deafen'd ear
Is by the tones of a loved voice caress'd—
A bolt is shot back somewhere in our breast,
And a lost pulse of feeling stirs again.
The eye sinks inward, and the heart lies plain,

And what we mean, we say, and what we would,
    we know!
A man becomes aware of his life's flow,
And hears its winding murmur, and he sees
The meadows where it glides, the sun, the breeze.

And there arrives a lull in the hot race
Wherein he doth for ever chase
That flying and elusive shadow, rest.
An air of coolness plays upon his face,
And an unwonted calm pervades his breast.
And then he thinks he knows
The hills where his life rose,
And the sea where it goes.

SONNETS.

1. *Quiet Work.*

ONE lesson, Nature, let me learn of thee,
　　One lesson, which in every wind is blown,
One lesson of two duties kept at one,
Though the loud world proclaim their enmity—

Of toil unsever'd from tranquillity !
Of labour, that in lasting fruit outgrows
Far noisier schemes, accomplish'd in repose—
Too great for haste, too high for rivalry !

Yes, while on earth a thousand discords ring,
Man's senseless uproar mingling with his toil,
Still do thy quiet ministers move on,

Their glorious tasks in silence perfecting !
Still working, blaming still our vain turmoil,
Labourers that shall not fail, when man is gone.

2. *To a Friend.*

WHO prop, thou ask'st, in these bad days, my
        mind?—
He much, the old man, who, clearest-soul'd of men,
Saw The Wide Prospect, and the Asian Fen,[5]
And Tmolus hill, and Smyrna bay, though blind.

Much he, whose friendship I not long since won,
That halting slave, who in Nicopolis
Taught Arrian, when Vespasian's brutal son
Clear'd Rome of what most shamed him.   But be his

My special thanks, whose even-balanced soul,
From first youth tested up to extreme old age,
Business could not make dull, nor passion wild;

Who saw life steadily, and saw it whole;
The mellow glory of the Attic stage,
Singer of sweet Colonus, and its child.

3. *Human Limits.*

ON SEEING GEORGE CRUIKSHANK'S PICTURE OF 'THE
BOTTLE,' IN THE COUNTRY.

A RTIST! whose hand, with horror wing'd, hath torn
     From the rank life of towns this leaf; and flung
The prodigy of full-blown crime among
Valleys and men to middle fortune born,

Not innocent, indeed, yet not forlorn;
Say, what shall calm us, when such guests intrude,
Like comets on the heavenly solitude?·
Shall breathless glades cheer'd by shy Dian's horn,

Cold-bubbling springs, or caves?—Not so! The soul
Breasts her own griefs; and, urged too fiercely, says:
'Why tremble? True, the nobleness of man

May be by man effaced; man can control
To pain, to death, the bent of his own days.
Know thou the worst! So much, not more, he *can*.'

4. *To a Republican Friend*, 1848.

GOD knows it, I am with you! If to prize
  Those virtues, prized and practised by too few,
But prized, but loved, but eminent in you,
Man's fundamental life; if to despise

The barren optimistic sophistries
Of comfortable moles, whom what they do
Teaches the limit of the just and true
(And for such doing they require no eyes);

If sadness at the long heart-wasting show
Wherein earth's great ones are disquieted;
If thoughts, not idle, while before me flow

The armies of the homeless and unfed—
If these are yours, if this is what you are,
Then am I yours, and what you feel, I share.

5. *Continued.*

YET, when I muse on what life is, I seem
  Rather to patience prompted, than that proud
Prospect of hope which France proclaims so loud—
France, famed in all great arts, in none supreme!

Seeing this vale, this earth, whereon we dream,
Is on all sides o'ershadow'd by the high
Uno'erleap'd mountains of necessity,
Sparing us narrower margin than we deem.

Nor will that day dawn at a human nod,
When, bursting through the network superposed
By selfish occupation—plot and plan,

Lust, avarice, envy—liberated man,
All difference with his fellow-mortal closed,
Shall be left standing face to face with God.

6. *East London.*

'TWAS August, and the fierce sun overhead
  Smote on the squalid streets of Bethnal Green,
And the pale weaver, through his windows seen
In Spitalfields, look'd thrice dispirited;

I met a preacher there I knew, and said:
'Ill and o'erwork'd, how fare you in this scene?'
'Bravely!' said he; 'for I of late have been
Much cheer'd with thoughts of Christ, *the living
    bread.'*

O human soul! as long as thou canst so
Set up a mark of everlasting light,
Above the howling senses' ebb and flow,

To cheer thee, and to right thee if thou roam,
Not with lost toil thou labourest through the night!
Thou mak'st the heaven thou hop'st indeed thy home.

7. *West London.*

CROUCH'D on the pavement, close by Belgrave
    Square,
A tramp I saw, ill, moody, and tongue-tied;
A babe was in her arms, and at her side
A girl; their clothes were rags, their feet were bare.

Some labouring men, whose work lay somewhere there,
Pass'd opposite; she touch'd her girl, who hied
Across, and begg'd, and came back satisfied;—
The rich she had let pass with frozen stare.

Thought I: 'Above her state this spirit towers;
She will not ask of aliens, but of friends,
Of sharers in a common human fate.

She turns from that cold succour, which attends
The unknown little from the unknowing great,
And points us to a better time ·than ours.'

8. *Worldly Place.*

*E*VEN *in a palace, life may be led well!*
    So spoke the imperial sage, purest of men,
Marcus Aurelius. - But the stifling den
Of common life, where, crowded up pell-mell,

Our freedom for a little bread we sell,
And drudge under some foolish master's ken,
Who rates us, if we peer outside our pen—
Match'd with a palace, is not this a hell?

Even in a palace! On his truth sincere,
Who spoke these words, no shadow ever came;
And when my ill-school'd spirit is aflame

Some nobler, ampler stage of life to win,
I'll stop, and say: 'There were no succour here!
The aids to noble life are all within.'

9. *Austerity of Poetry.*

THAT son of Italy who tried to blow,[6]
Ere Dante came, the trump of sacred song,
In his light youth amid a festal throng
Sate with his bride to see a public show.

Fair was the bride, and on her front did glow
Youth like a star; and what to youth belong,
Gay raiment, sparkling gauds, elation strong.
A prop gave way! crash fell a platform! lo,

Mid struggling sufferers, hurt to death, she lay!
Shuddering, they drew her garments off—and found
A robe of sackcloth next the smooth, white skin.

Such, poets, is your bride, the Muse! young, gay,
Radiant, adorn'd outside; a hidden ground
Of thought and of austerity within.

10. *Religious Isolation.*

TO A FRIEND.

CHILDREN (as such forgive them!) have I known,
　　Ever in their own eager pastime bent
To make the incurious bystander, intent
On his own swarming thoughts, an interest own;

Too fearful or too fond to play alone.
Do thou, whom light in thine own inmost soul
(Not less thy boast) illuminates, control
Wishes unworthy of a man full-grown!

What though the holy secret which moulds thee
Moulds not the solid earth? though never winds
Have whisper'd it to the complaining sea,

Nature's great law, and law of all men's minds?—
To its own impulse every creature stirs;
Live by thy light, and earth will live by hers!

11. *East and West.*

IN the bare midst of Anglesey they show
   Two springs which close by one another play,
And, 'Thirteen hundred years agone,' they say,
'Two saints met often where those waters flow.

One came from Penmon, westward, and a glow
Whiten'd his face from the sun's fronting ray;
Eastward the other, from the dying day—
And he with unsunn'd face did always go.'

Seiriol the Bright, Kybi the Dark! men said.
The seër from the East was then in light,
The seër from the West was then in shade.

Ah! now 'tis changed. In conquering sunshine
     bright
The man of the bold West now comes array'd;
He of the mystic East is touch'd with night.

12. *The Better Part.*

LONG fed on boundless hopes, O race of man,
  How angrily thou spurn'st all simpler fare!
'Christ,' some one says, 'was human as we are.
No judge eyes us from Heaven, our sin to scan.

We live no more, when we have done our span.'—
'Well, then, for Christ,' thou answerest, 'who can care?
From sin, which Heaven records not, why forbear?
Live we like brutes our life without a plan!'

So answerest thou; but why not rather say:
'Hath man no second life?—*Pitch this one high!*
Sits there no judge in Heaven, our sin to see?—

More strictly, then, the inward judge obey!
Was Christ a man like us?—*Ah! let us try
If we then, too, can be such men as he!'*

13. *The Good Shepherd with the Kid.*

*H*E saves the sheep, the goats he doth not save !
    So rang Tertullian's sentence, on the side
Of that unpitying Phrygian sect which cried:[7]
'Him can no fount of fresh forgiveness lave,

Who sins, once wash'd by the baptismal wave !'
So spake the fierce Tertullian. But she sigh'd,
The infant Church ! of love she felt the tide
Stream on her from her Lord's yet recent grave.

And then she smiled; and in the Catacombs,
With eye suffused but heart inspired true,
On those walls subterranean, where she hid

Her head in ignominy, death, and tombs,
She her Good Shepherd's hasty image drew—
And on his shoulders, not a lamb, a kid.

14.　*The Divinity.*

'YES, write it in the rock,' Saint Bernard said,
　'Grave it on brass with adamantine pen!
'Tis God himself becomes apparent, when
God's wisdom and God's goodness are display'd,

For God of these his attributes is made.'—
Well spake the impetuous Saint, and bore of men
The suffrage captive; now, not one in ten
Recalls the obscure opposer he outweigh'd.[8]

God's wisdom and *God's goodness !*—Ay, but fools
Mis-define these till God knows them no more.
Wisdom and goodness, they are God!—what schools

Have yet so much as heard this simpler lore?
This no Saint preaches, and this no Church rules;
'Tis in the desert, now and heretofore.

15. *Immortality.*

FOIL'D by our fellow-men, depress'd, outworn,
    We leave the brutal world to take its way,
And, *Patience! in another life*, we say,
The world shall be thrust down, and we up-borne!

And will not, then, the immortal armies scorn
The world's poor, routed leavings? or will they,
Who fail'd under the heat of this life's day,
Support the fervours of the heavenly morn?

No, no! the energy of life may be
Kept on after the grave, but not begun!
And he who flagg'd not in the earthly strife,

From strength to strength advancing—only he,
His soul well-knit, and all his battles won,
Mounts, and that hardly, to eternal life.

16. *Monica's Last Prayer.*[9]

' OH could thy grave at home, at Carthage, be !' —
   Care not for that, and lay me where I fall !
Everywhere heard will be the judgment-call.
But at God's altar, oh ! remember me.

Thus Monica, and died in Italy.
Yet fervent had her longing been, through all
Her course, for home at last, and burial
With her own husband, by the Libyan sea.

Had been! but at the end, to her pure soul
All tie with all beside seem'd vain and cheap,
And union before God the only care.

Creeds pass, rites change, no altar standeth whole!
Yet we her memory, as she pray'd, will keep,
Keep by this : *Life in God, and union there !*

HUMAN LIFE.

WHAT mortal, when he saw,
  Life's voyage done, his heavenly Friend,
Could ever yet dare tell him fearlessly :
'I have kept uninfringed my nature's law ;
The inly-written chart thou gavest me
To guide me, I have steer'd by to the end ?'

Ah! let us make no claim
On life's incognisable sea
To too exact a steering of our way !
Let us not fret and fear to miss our aim,
If some fair coast has lured us to make stay,
Or some friend hail'd us to keep company !—

Ay, we would each fain drive
At random, and not steer by rule !
Weakness ! and worse, weakness bestow'd in vain !
Winds from our side the unsuiting consort rive,
We rush by coasts where we had lief remain ;
Man cannot, though he would, live chance's fool.

No! as the foaming swath
Of torn-up water, on the main,
Falls heavily away with long-drawn roar
On either side the black deep-furrow'd path
Cut by an onward-labouring vessel's prore,
And never touches the ship-side again ;

Even so we leave behind—
As, charter'd by some unknown Powers,
We stem across the sea by night—
The joys which were not for our use design'd,
The friends to whom we had no natural right,
The homes that were not.destined to be ours.

RESIGNATION.

*T*O die be given us, or attain !
  Fierce work it were, to do again.
So pilgrims, bound for Mecca, pray'd
At burning noon; so warriors said,
Scarf'd with the cross, who watch'd the miles
Of dust that wreathed their struggling files
Down Lydian mountains; so, when snows
Round Alpine summits eddying rose,
The Goth, bound Rome-wards; so the Hun,
Crouch'd on his saddle, when the sun
Went lurid down o'er flooded plains
Through which the groaning Danube strains
To the drear Euxine;—so pray all,
Whom labours, self-ordain'd, enthrall;
Because they to themselves propose
On this side the all-common close
A goal which, gain'd, may give repose.
So pray they; and to stand again
Where they stood once, to them were pain;

Pain to thread back and to renew
Past straits, and currents long steer'd through.

But milder natures, and more free;
Whom an unblamed serenity
Hath freed from passions, and the state
Of struggle these necessitate;
Whom schooling of the stubborn mind
Hath made, or birth hath found, resign'd—
These mourn not, that their goings pay
Obedience to the passing day.
These claim not every laughing Hour
For handmaid to their striding power;
Each in her turn, with torch uprear'd,
To await their march; and when appear'd,
Through the cold gloom, with measured race,
To usher for a destined space,
(Her own sweet errands all forgone)
The too imperious traveller on!
These, Fausta, ask not this; nor thou,
Time's chafing prisoner, ask it now!

We left, just ten years since, you say,
That wayside inn we left to-day.[10]

Our jovial host, as forth we fare,
Shouts greeting from his easy chair;
High on a bank our leader stands,
Reviews and ranks his motley bands,
Makes clear our goal to every eye—
The valley's western boundary.
A gate swings to! our tide hath flow'd
Already from the silent road!
The valley-pastures, one by one,
Are threaded, quiet in the sun;
And now beyond the rude stone bridge
Slopes gracious up the western ridge.
Its woody border, and the last
Of its dark upland farms is past;
Cool farms, with open-lying stores,
Under their burnish'd sycamores—
All past! and through the trees we glide
Emerging on the green hill-side.
There climbing hangs, a far-seen sign,
Our wavering, many-colour'd line;
There winds, upstreaming slowly still
Over the summit of the hill.
And now, in front, behold outspread
Those upper regions we must tread!

Mild hollows, and clear heathy swells,
The cheerful silence of the fells.
Some two hours' march, with serious air,
Through the deep noontide heats we fare;
The red-grouse, springing at our sound,
Skims, now and then, the shining ground;
No life, save his and ours, intrudes
Upon these breathless solitudes.
O joy! again the farms appear!
Cool shade is there, and rustic cheer;
There springs the brook will guide us down,
Bright comrade, to the noisy town.
Lingering, we follow down! we gain
The town, the highway, and the plain.
And many a mile of dusty way,
Parch'd and road-worn, we made that day;
But, Fausta! I remember well
That as the balmy darkness fell
We bathed our hands with speechless glee,
That night, in the wide-glimmering sea.

Once more we tread this self-same road,
Fausta! which ten years since we trod;
Alone we tread it, you and I,

Ghosts of that boisterous company.
Here, where the brook shines, near its head,
In its clear, shallow, turf-fringed bed;
Here, whence the eye first sees, far down,
Capp'd with faint smoke, the noisy town;
Here sit we, and again unroll,
Though slowly, the familiar whole!
The solemn wastes of heathy hill
Sleep in the July sunshine still;
The self-same shadows now, as then,
Play through this grassy upland glen;
The loose dark stones on the green way
Lie strewn, it seems, where then they lay;
On this mild bank above the stream,
(You crush them) the blue gentians gleam!
Still this· wild brook, the rushes cool,
The sailing foam, the shining pool—
These are not changed; and we, you say,
Are scarce more changed, in truth, than they.

The gipsies, whom we met below,
They, too, have long roam'd to and fro;
They ramble, leaving, where they pass,
Their fragments on the cumber'd grass.

And often to some kindly place
Chance guides the migratory race,
Where, though long wanderings intervene,
They recognise a former scene.
The dingy tents are pitch'd; the fires
Give to the wind their wavering spires;
In dark knots crouch round the wild flame
Their children, as when first they came;
They see their shackled beasts again
Move, browsing, up the grey-wall'd lane.
Signs are not wanting, which might raise
The ghosts in them of former days;
Signs are not wanting, if they would;
Suggestions to disquietude!
For them, for all, time's busy touch,
While it mends little, troubles much;
Their joints grow stiffer—but the year
Runs his old round of dubious cheer;
Chilly they grow—yet winds in March,
Still, sharp as ever, freeze and parch;
They must live still—and yet, God knows,
Crowded and keen the country grows!
It seems as if, in their decay,
The law grew stronger every day!

So might they reason; so compare,
Fausta! times past with times that are.
But no!—they rubb'd through yesterday
In their hereditary way;
And they will rub through, if they can,
To-morrow on the self-same plan;
Till death arrives to supersede,
For them, vicissitude and need.

The poet, to whose mighty heart
Heaven doth a quicker pulse impart,
Subdues that energy to scan
Not his own course, but that of man.
Though he move mountains; though his day
Be pass'd on the proud heights of sway;
Though he hath loosed a thousand chains;
Though he hath borne immortal pains;
Action and suffering though he know—
He hath not lived, if he lives so!
He sees, in some great-historied land,
A ruler of the people stand,
Sees his strong thought in fiery flood
Roll through the heaving multitude;
Exults—yet for no moment's space

Envies the all-regarded place.
Beautiful eyes meet his—and he
Bears to admire uncravingly;
They pass—he, mingled with the crowd,
Is in their far-off triumphs proud.
From some high station he looks down,
At sunset, on a populous town;
Surveys each happy group which fleets,
Toil ended, through the shining streets,
Each with some errand of its own—
And does not say, *I am alone !*
He sees the gentle stir of birth
When morning purifies the earth;
He leans upon a gate, and sees
The pastures, and the quiet trees.
Low woody hill, with gracious bound,
Folds the still valley almost round;
The cuckoo, loud on some high lawn,
Is answer'd from the depth of dawn;
In the hedge straggling to the stream,
Pale, dew-drench'd, half-shut roses gleam;
But where the further side slopes down
He sees the drowsy new-waked clown
In his white quaint-embroider'd frock
Make, whistling, toward his mist-wreath'd flock—

Slowly, behind his heavy tread,
The wet flower'd grass heaves up its head.
Lean'd on his gate, he gazes! tears
Are in his eyes, and in his ears
The murmur of a thousand years.
Before him he sees life unroll,
A placid and continuous whole;
That general life, which does not cease,
Whose secret is not joy, but peace;
That life, whose dumb wish is not miss'd
If birth proceeds, if things subsist;
The life of plants, and stones, and rain—
The life he craves! if not in vain
Fate gave, what chance shall not control,
His sad lucidity of soul.

You listen!—but that wandering smile,
Fausta, betrays you cold the while!
Your eyes pursue the bells of foam
Wash'd, eddying, from this bank, their home.
Those gipsies, so your thoughts I scan,
Are less, the poet more, than man;
They feel not, though they move and see!
Deeply the poet feels! but he
Breathes, when he will, immortal air,

Where Orpheus and where Homer are.
In the day's life, whose iron round
Hems us all in, he is not bound ;
He escapes thence, but we abide.
Not deep the poet sees, but wide !

The world in which we live and move
Outlasts aversion, outlasts love ;
Outlasts each effort, interest, hope,
Remorse, grief, joy ;—and were the scope
Of these affections wider made,
Man still would see, and see dismay'd,
Beyond his passion's widest range
Far regions of eternal change.
Nay, and since death, which wipes out man,
Finds him with many an unsolved plan,
With much unknown, and much untried,
Wonder not dead, and thirst not dried,
Still gazing on the ever full
Eternal mundane spectacle ;
This world in which we draw our breath,
In some sense, Fausta ! outlasts death.

Blame thou not therefore him, who dares
Judge vain beforehand human cares ;
Whose natural insight can discern

What through experience others learn;
Who needs not love and power, to know
Love transient, power an unreal show;
Who treads at ease life's uncheer'd ways—
Him blame not, Fausta, rather praise!
Rather thyself for some aim pray
Nobler than this, to fill the day!
Rather, that heart, which burns in thee,
Ask, not to amuse, but to set free!
Be passionate hopes not ill resign'd
For quiet, and a fearless mind!
And though fate grudge to thee and me
The poet's rapt security,
Yet they, believe me, who await
No gifts from chance, have conquer'd fate.
They, winning room to see and hear,
And to men's business not too near,
Through clouds of individual strife
Draw homeward to the general life.
Like leaves by suns not yet uncurl'd—
To the wise, foolish; to the world,
Weak;—yet not weak, I might reply,
Not foolish, Fausta! in His eye,
To whom each moment in its race,
Crowd as we will its neutral space,

Is but a quiet watershed
Whence, equally, the seas of life and death are fed.

Enough, we live !—and if a life,
With large results so little rife,
Though bearable, seem hardly worth
This pomp of worlds, this pain of birth;
Yet, Fausta! the mute turf we tread,
The solemn hills around us spread,
This stream which falls incessantly,
The strange-scrawl'd rocks, the lonely sky,
If I might lend their life a voice,
Seem to bear rather than rejoice.
And even could the intemperate prayer
Man iterates, while these forbear,
For movement, for an ampler sphere,
Pierce Fate's impenetrable ear;
Not milder is the general lot
Because our spirits have forgot,
In action's dizzying eddy whirl'd,
The something that infects the world.

EPILOGUE TO
LESSING'S LAOCOÖN.

ONE morn as through Hyde Park we walk'd,
　　My friend and I, by chance we talk'd
Of Lessing's famed Laocoön;
And after we awhile had gone
In Lessing's track, and tried to see
What painting is, what poetry—
Diverging to another thought,
'Ah,' cries my friend, 'but who hath taught
Why music and the other arts　　　．
Oftener perform aright their parts
Than poetry? why she, than they,
Fewer fine successes can display?

'For 'tis so, surely! Even in Greece,
Where best the poet framed his piece,
Even in that Phœbus-guarded ground
Pausanias on his travels found

Good poems, if he look'd, more rare
(Though many) than good statues were—
For these, in truth, were everywhere !
Of bards full many a stroke divine
In Dante's, Petrarch's, Tasso's line,
The land of Ariosto show'd ;
And yet, e'en there, the canvas glow'd
With triumphs, a yet ampler brood,
Of Raphael and his brotherhood.
And nobly perfect, in our day
Of haste, half-work, and disarray,
Profound yet touching, sweet yet strong,
Hath risen Goethe's, Wordsworth's song ;
Yet even I (and none will bow
Deeper to these !) must needs allow,
They yield us not, to soothe our pains,
Such multitude of heavenly strains
As from the kings of sound are blown,
Mozart, Beethoven, Mendelssohn.'

While thus my friend discoursed, we pass
Out of the path, and take the grass.
The grass had still the green of May,
And still the unblacken'd elms were gay ;

The kine were resting in the shade,
The flies a summer murmur made.
Bright was the morn and south the air;
The soft-couch'd cattle were as fair
As those which pastured by the sea,
That old-world morn, in Sicily,
When on the beach the Cyclops lay,
And Galatea from the bay
Mock'd her poor lovelorn giant's lay.
'Behold,' I said, 'the painter's sphere!
The limits of his art appear!
The passing group, the summer morn,
The grass, the elms, that blossom'd thorn;
Those cattle couch'd, or, as they rise,
Their shining flanks, their liquid eyes;
These, or much greater things, but caught
Like these, and in one aspect brought.
In outward semblance he must give
A moment's life of things that live;
Then let him choose his moment well,
With power divine its story tell!'

Still we walk'd on, in thoughtful mood,
And now upon the bridge we stood.

Full of sweet breathings was the air,
Of sudden stirs and pauses fair.
Down o'er the stately bridge the breeze
Came rustling from the garden-trees,
And on the sparkling waters play'd;
Light-plashing waves an answer made,
And mimic boats their haven near'd.
Beyond, the Abbey-towers appear'd,
By mist and chimneys unconfined,
Free to the sweep of light and wind;
While, through their earth-moor'd nave below,
Another breath of wind doth blow,
Sound as of wandering breeze—but sound
In laws by human artists bound.
'The world of music!' I exclaim'd,
'This breeze that rustles by, that famed
Abbey recall it! what a sphere,
Large and profound, hath genius here!
The inspired musician what a range,
What power of passion, wealth of change!
Some source of feeling he must choose
And its lock'd fount of beauty use,
And through the stream of music tell
Its else unutterable spell;

To choose it rightly is his part,
And press into its inmost heart.

Miserere, Domine !
The words are utter'd, and they flee.
Deep is their penitential moan,
Mighty their pathos, but 'tis gone !
They have declared the spirit's sore
Sore load, and words can do no more.
Beethoven takes them then—those two
Poor, bounded words !—and makes them new ;
Infinite makes them, makes them young,
Transplants them to another tongue
Where they can now, without constraint,
Pour all the soul of their complaint,
And roll adown a channel large
The wealth divine they have in charge.
Page after page of music turn,
And still they live and still they burn,
Perennial, passion-fraught, and free—
Miserere, Domine !'

Onward we moved, and reach'd the ride
Where gaily flows the human tide.

Afar, in rest the cattle lay;
We heard, afar, faint music play;
But agitated, brisk, and near,
Men, with their stream of life, were here.
Some hang upon the rails, and some,
On foot, behind them, go and come.
This through the ride upon his steed
Goes slowly by, and this at speed;
The young, the happy, and the fair,
The old, the sad, the worn were there;
Some vacant, and some musing went,
And some in talk and merriment.
Nods, smiles, and greetings, and farewells !
And now and then, perhaps, there swells
A sigh, a tear—but in the throng
All changes fast, and hies along;
Hies, ah, from whence, what native ground?
And to what goal, what ending, bound?
'Behold at last the poet's sphere !
But who,' I said, 'suffices here?

For, ah ! so much he has to do !
Be painter and musician too !
The aspect of the moment show,

The feeling of the moment know!
The aspect not, I grant, express
Clear as the painter's art can dress;
The feeling not, I grant, explore
So deep as the musician's lore—
But clear as words can make revealing,
And deep as words can follow feeling.
But, ah, then comes his sorest spell
Of toil! he must life's *movement* tell!
The thread which binds it all in one,
And not its separate parts alone!
The *movement* he must tell of life,
Its pain and pleasure, rest and strife;
His eye must travel down, at full,
The long, unpausing spectacle;
With faithful unrelaxing force
Attend it from its primal source,
From change to change and year to year
Attend it of its mid career,
Attend it to the last repose
And solemn silence of its close.

The cattle rising from the grass
His thought must follow where they pass;

The penitent with anguish bow'd
His thought must follow through the crowd.
Yes, all this eddying, motley throng
That sparkles in the sun along,
Girl, statesman, merchant, soldier bold,
Master and servant, young and old,
Grave, gay, child, parent, husband, wife,
He follows home, and lives their life!

And many, many are the souls
Life's movement fascinates, controls;
It draws them on, they cannot save
Their feet from its alluring wave;
They cannot leave it, they must go
With its unconquerable flow.
But, ah, how few of all that try
This mighty march, do aught but die!
For ill endow'd for such a way,
Ill stored in strength, in wits, are they!
They faint, they stagger to and fro,
And wandering from the stream they go;
In pain, in terror, in distress,
They see, all round, a wilderness.
Sometimes a momentary gleam

They catch of the mysterious stream;
Sometimes, a second's space, their ear
The murmur of its waves doth hear;
That transient glimpse in song they say,
But not as painter can pourtray!
That transient sound in song they tell,
But not, as the musician, well!
And when at last their snatches cease,
And they are silent and at peace,
The stream of life's majestic whole
Hath ne'er been mirror'd on their soul.

Only a few the life-stream's shore
With safe unwandering feet explore;
Untired its movement bright attend,
Follow its windings to the end.
Then from its brimming waves their eye
Drinks up delighted ecstasy,
And its deep-toned, melodious voice,
For ever makes their ear rejoice.
They speak! the happiness divine
They feel, runs o'er in every line;
Its spell is round them like a shower;
It gives them pathos, gives them power.

No painter yet hath such a way,
Nor no musician made, as they;
And gather'd on immortal knolls
Such lovely flowers for cheering souls.
Beethoven, Raphael, cannot reach
The charm which Homer, Shakspeare, teach.
To these, to these, their thankful race
Gives, then, the first, the fairest place!
And brightest is their glory's sheen,
For greatest has their labour been.'

THE YOUTH OF NATURE.

R AISED are the dripping oars!
    Silent the boat! the lake,
Lovély and soft as a dream,
Swims in the sheen of the moon.
The mountains stand at its head
Clear in the pure June night,
But the valleys are flooded with haze.
Rydal and Fairfield are there!
In the shadow Wordsworth lies dead.
So it is, so it will be for aye!
Nature is fresh as of old,
Is lovely; a mortal is dead.

The spots which recall him survive,
For he lent a new life to these hills.
The Pillar still broods o'er the fields
Which border Ennerdale Lake,
And Egremont sleeps by the sea.
The gleam of The Evening Star

Twinkles on Grasmere no more,
But ruin'd and solemn and grey
The sheepfold of Michael survives,
And far to the south, the heath
Still blows in the Quantock coombs,
By the favourite waters of Ruth.
These survive! yet not without pain,
Pain and dejection to-night,
Can I feel that their poet is gone.

He grew old in an age he condemn'd.
He look'd on the rushing decay
Of the times which had shelter'd his youth;
Felt the dissolving throes
Of a social order he loved;
Outlived his brethren, his peers;
And, like the Theban seer,
Died in his enemies' day.

Cold bubbled the spring of Tilphusa,
Copais lay bright in the moon,
Helicon glass'd in the lake
Its firs, and afar, rose the peaks
Of Parnassus, snowily clear;

Thebes was behind him in flames,
And the clang of arms in his ear,
When his awe-struck captors led
The Theban seer to the spring.
Tiresias drank and died.
Nor did reviving Thebes
See such a prophet again.

Well may we mourn, when the head
Of a sacred poet lies low
In an age which can rear them no more!
The complaining millions of men
Darken in labour and pain;
But he was a priest to us all
Of the wonder and bloom of the world,
Which we saw with his eyes, and were glad.
He is dead, and the fruit-bearing day
Of his· race is past on the earth;
And darkness returns to our eyes.

For oh! is it you, is it you,
Moonlight, and shadow, and lake,
And mountains, that fill us with joy,
Or the poet who sings you so well?

Is it you, O beauty, O grace,
O charm, O romance, that we feel,
Or the voice which reveals what you are
Are ye, like daylight and sun,
Shared and rejoiced in by all?
Or are ye immersed in the mass
Of matter, and hard to extract,
Or sunk at the core of the world
Too deep for the most to discern?
Like stars in the deep of the sky,
Which arise on the glass of the sage,
But are lost when their watcher is gone.

'They are here'—I heard, as men heard
In Mysian Ida the voice
Of the Mighty Mother, or Crete,
The murmur of Nature reply:—
'Loveliness, magic, and grace,
They are here! they are set in the world!
They abide! and the finest of souls
Has not been thrill'd by them all,
Nor the dullest been dead to them quite.
The poet who sings them may die,
But they are immortal, and live,

For they are the life of the world!
Will ye not learn it, and know,
When ye mourn that a poet is dead,
That the singer was less than his themes,
Life, and emotion, and I?

More than the singer are these!
Weak is the tremor of pain
That thrills in his mournfullest chord
To that which once ran through his soul.
Cold the elation of joy
In his gladdest, airiest song,
To that which of old in his youth
Fill'd him and made him divine.
Hardly his voice at its best
Gives us a sense of the awe,
The vastness, the grandeur, the gloom
Of the unlit gulph of himself.

Ye know not yourselves! and your bards,
The clearest, the best, who have read
Most in themselves, have beheld
Less than they left unreveal'd.
Ye express not yourselves!—can ye make

With marble, with colour, with word,
What charm'd you in others re-live?
Can thy pencil, O artist! restore
The figure, the bloom of thy love,
As she was in her morning of spring?
Canst thou paint the ineffable smile
Of her eyes as they rested on thine?
Can the image of life have the glow,
The motion of life itself?

Yourselves and your fellows ye know not! and me
The mateless, the one, will ye know?
Will ye scan me, and read me, and tell
Of the thoughts that ferment in my breast,
My longing, my sadness, my joy?
Will ye claim for your great ones the gift
To have render'd the gleam of my skies,
To have echoed the moan of my seas,
Utter'd the voice of my hills?
When your great ones depart, will ye say:
All things have suffered a loss!
Nature is hid in their grave!

Race after race, man after man,

Have thought that my secret was theirs,
Have dream'd that I lived but for them,
That they were my glory and joy.—
They are dust, they are changed, they are gone !
   I remain !'

THE YOUTH OF MAN.

WE, O Nature, depart;
    Thou survivest us! this,
This, I know, is the law.
Yes, but more than this,
Thou who seest us die
Seest us change while we live;
Seest our dreams, one by one,
Seest our errors depart;
Watchest us, Nature, throughout,
Mild and inscrutably calm!

Well for us that we change!
Well for us that the power
Which in our morning prime
Saw the mistakes of our youth,
Sweet, and forgiving, and good,
Sees the contrition of age!

Behold, O Nature, this pair !
See them to-night where they stand,
Not with the halo of youth
Crowning their brows with its light,
Not with the sunshine of hope,
Not with the rapture of spring,
Which they had of old, when they stood
Years ago at my side
In this self-same garden, and said :
'We are young, and the world is ours,
For man is the king of the world !
Fools that these mystics are
Who prate of Nature ! but she
Hath neither beauty, nor warmth,
Nor life, nor emotion, nor power.
But man has a thousand gifts,
And the generous dreamer invests
The senseless world with them all.
Nature is nothing ! her charm
Lives in our eyes which can paint,
Lives in our hearts which can feel !'

Thou, O Nature, wast mute,
Mute as of old ! days flew,

Days and years; and Time
With the ceaseless stroke of his wings
Brush'd off the bloom from their soul.
Clouded and dim grew their eye,
Languid their heart—for youth
Quicken'd its pulses no more.
Slowly within the walls
Of an ever-narrowing world
They droop'd, they grew blind, they grew old.
Thee and their youth in thee,
Nature, they saw no more!

Murmur of living!
Stir of existence!
Soul of the world!
Make, oh make yourselves felt
To the dying spirit of youth!
Come, like the breath of the spring!
Leave not a human soul
To grow old in darkness and pain!
Only the living can feel you,
But leave us not while we live!

Here they stand to-night—

Here, where this grey balustrade
Crowns the still valley; behind
Is the castled house with its woods
Which shelter'd their childhood, the sun
On its ivied windows! a scent
From the grey-wall'd gardens, a breath
Of the fragrant stock and the pink,
Perfumes the evening air.
Their children play on the lawns.
They stand and listen; they hear
The children's shouts, and, at times,
Faintly, the bark of a dog
From a distant farm in the hills;—
Nothing besides! in front
The wide, wide valley outspreads
To the dim horizon, reposed
In the twilight, and bathed in dew,
Corn-field and hamlet and copse
Darkening fast! but a light,
Far off, a glory of day,
Still plays on the city-spires;
And there in the dusk by the walls,
With the grey mist marking its course
Through the silent flowery land,

On, to the plains, to the sea,
Floats the imperial stream.

Well I know what they feel !
They gaze, and the evening wind
Plays on their faces ! they gaze ;
Airs from the Eden of youth
Awake and stir in their soul !
The past returns ; they feel
What they are, alas, what they were !
They, not Nature, are changed !
Well I know what they feel.

Hush ! for tears
Begin to steal to their eyes ;
Hush ! for fruit
Grows from such sorrow as theirs.

And they remember,
With piercing, untold anguish,
The proud boasting of their youth ;
And they feel how Nature was fair ;
And the mists of delusion,
And the scales of habit,

Fall away from their eyes;
And they see, for a moment,
Stretching out, like the desert
In its weary, unprofitable length,
Their faded, ignoble lives.

While the locks are yet brown on thy head,
While the soul still looks through thine eyes,
While the heart still pours
The mantling blood to thy cheek,
Sink, O youth, in thy soul!
Yearn to the greatness of Nature!
Rally the good in the depths of thyself!

YOUTH AND CALM.

'TIS death! and peace, indeed, is here,
  And ease from shame, and rest from fear.
There's nothing can dismarble now
The smoothness of that limpid brow.
But is a calm like this, in truth,
The crowning end of life and youth,
And when this boon rewards the dead,
Are all debts paid, has all been said?
And is the heart of youth so light,
Its step so firm, its eye so bright,
Because on its hot brow there blows
A wind of promise and repose
From the far grave, to which it goes;
Because it has the hope to come,
One day, to harbour in the tomb?
Ah no, the bliss youth dreams is one
For daylight, for the cheerful sun,
For feeling nerves and living breath—
Youth dreams a bliss on this side death!

It dreams a rest, if not more deep,
More grateful than this marble sleep;
It hears a voice within it tell:
Calm's not life's crown, though calm is well!
'Tis all perhaps which man acquires,
But 'tis not what our youth desires.

YOUTH'S AGITATIONS.

WHEN I shall be divorced, some ten years hence,
　　From this poor present self which I am now;
When youth has done its tedious vain expense
Of passions that for ever ebb and flow;

Shall I not joy youth's heats are left behind,
And breathe more happy in an even clime?
Ah no! for then I shall begin to find
A thousand virtues in this hated time.

Then I shall wish its agitations back,
And all its thwarting currents of desire;
Then I shall praise the heat which then I lack,
And call this hurrying fever, generous fire;

And sigh that one thing only has been lent
To youth and age in common—discontent.

THE WORLD'S TRIUMPHS.

SO far as I conceive the world's rebuke
   To him address'd who would recast her new,
Not from herself her fame of strength she took,
But from their weakness, who would work her rue.

'Behold,' she cries, 'so many rages lull'd,
So many fiery spirits quite cool'd down!
Look how so many valours, long undull'd,
After short commerce with me, fear my frown!

Thou too, when thou against my crimes wouldst cry,
Let thy foreboded homage check thy tongue!'—
The world speaks well; yet might her foe reply:
'Are wills so weak?—then let not mine wait long!

Hast thou so rare a poison?—let me be
Keener to slay thee, lest thou poison me!'

GROWING OLD.

WHAT is it to grow old?
    Is it to lose the glory of the form,
The lustre of the eye?
Is it for beauty to forego her wreath?—
Yes, but not this alone!

Is it to feel our strength—
Not our bloom only, but our strength—decay?
Is it to feel each limb
Grow stiffer, every function less exact,
Each nerve more weakly strung?

Yes, this, and more! but not,
Ah, 'tis not what in youth we dream'd 'twould be!
'Tis not to have our life
Mellow'd and soften'd as with sunset-glow,
A golden day's decline!

'Tis not to see the world
As from a height, with rapt prophetic eyes,
And heart profoundly stirr'd ;
And weep, and feel the fulness of the past,
The years that are no more !

It is to spend long days
And not once feel that we were ever young !
It is to add, immured
In the hot prison of the present, month
To month with weary pain.

It is to suffer this,
And feel but half, and feebly, what we feel.
Deep in our hidden heart
Festers the dull remembrance of a change,
But no emotion—none !

It is—last stage of all—
When we are frozen up within, and quite
The phantom of ourselves,
To hear the world applaud the hollow ghost
Which blamed the living man.

DESPONDENCY.

THE thoughts that rain their steady glow
    Like stars on life's cold sea,
Which others know, or say they know—
They never shone for me!

Thoughts light, like gleams, my spirit's sky,
But they will not remain;
They light me once, they hurry by,
And never come again.

SELF-DECEPTION.

SAY, what blinds us, that we claim the glory
    Of possessing powers not our share?—
Since man woke on earth, he knows his story,
But, before we woke on earth, we were.

Long, long since, undower'd yet, our spirit
Roam'd, ere birth, the treasuries of God;
Saw the gifts, the powers it might inherit,
Ask'd an outfit for its earthly road.

Then, as now, this tremulous, eager being
Strain'd, and long'd, and grasp'd each gift it saw;
Then, as now, a power beyond our seeing
Staved us back, and gave our choice the law.

Ah, whose hand that day through Heaven guided
Man's new spirit, since it was not we?
Ah, who sway'd our choice, and who decided
What our gifts, and what our wants should be?

For, alas, he left us each retaining
Shreds of gifts which he refused in full!
Still these waste us with their hopeless straining;
Still the attempt to use them proves them null.

And on earth we wander, groping, reeling;
Powers stir in us, stir and disappear.
Ah, and he, who placed our master-feeling,
Fail'd to place that master-feeling clear!

We but dream we have our wish'd-for powers,
Ends we seek we never shall attain!
Ah! *some* power exists there, which is ours?
Some end is there, we indeed may gain?

THE PROGRESS OF POESY.

A Variation.

YOUTH rambles on life's arid mount,
  And strikes the rock, and finds the vein,
And brings the water from the fount,
The fount which shall not flow again.

The man mature with labour chops
For the bright stream a channel grand,
And sees not that the sacred drops
Ran off and vanish'd out of hand.

And then the old man totters nigh,
And feebly rakes among the stones.
The mount is mute, the channel dry!
And down he lays his weary bones.

THE LAST WORD.

CREEP into thy narrow bed,
  Creep, and let no more be said.
Vain thy onset! all stands fast!
Thou thyself must break at last.

Let the long contention cease!
Geese are swans, and swans are geese.
Let them have it how they will!
Thou art tired; best be still.

They out-talk'd thee, hiss'd thee, tore thee?
Better men fared thus before thee!
Fired their ringing shot and pass'd,
Hotly charged—and broke at last.

Charge once more, then, and be dumb!
Let the victors, when they come,
When the forts of folly fall,
Find thy body by the wall!

A NAMELESS EPITAPH.

ASK not my name, O friend!
That Being only, which hath known each man
From the beginning, can
Remember each unto the end.

THE SECOND BEST.

MODERATE tasks and moderate leisure,
   Quiet living, strict-kept measure
Both in suffering and in pleasure—
   'Tis for this thy nature yearns.

But so many books thou readest,
But so many schemes thou breedest,
But so many wishes feedest,
   That thy poor head almost turns.

And (the world's so madly jangled,
Human things so fast entangled)
Nature's wish must now be strangled
   For that best which she discerns.

So it *must* be! yet, while leading
A strain'd life, while overfeeding,
Like the rest, his wit with reading,
   No small profit that man earns,

Who through all he meets can steer him,
Can reject what cannot clear him,
Cling to what can truly cheer him!
  Who each day more surely learns

That an impulse, from the distance
Of his deepest, best existence,
To the words, ' Hope, Light, Persistence,'
  Strongly sets and truly burns!

PIS-ALLER.

'MAN is blind because of sin;
         Revelation makes him sure.
Without that, who looks within,
Looks in vain, for all's obscure.'

Nay, look closer into man!
Tell me, can you find indeed
Nothing sure, no moral plan
Clear prescribed, without your creed?

'No, I nothing can perceive!
Without that, all's dark for men.
That, or nothing, I believe.'—
For God's sake, believe it then!

IN UTRUMQUE PARATUS.

IF, in the silent mind of One all-pure
    At first imagined lay
The sacred world, and by procession sure
From those still deeps, in form and colour drest,
Seasons alternating and night and day,
The long-mused thought to north, south, east, and
        west,
    Took then its all-seen way;

O waking on a world which thus-wise springs!
    Whether it needs thee count
Betwixt thy waking and the birth of things
Ages or hours—O waking on life's stream!
By lonely pureness to the all-pure fount
(Only by this thou canst) the colour'd dream
    Of life remount!

Thin, thin the pleasant human noises grow,
     And faint the city gleams,
Rare the lone pastoral huts;—marvel not thou!
The solemn peaks but to the stars are known,
But to the stars, and the cold lunar beams;
Alone the sun arises, and alone
     Spring the great streams.

But if the wild unfather'd mass no birth
     In divine seats hath known;
In the blank, echoing solitude if Earth,
Rocking her obscure body to and fro,
Ceases not from all time to heave and groan,
Unfruitful oft, and, at her happiest throe,
     Forms, what she forms, alone;

O seeming sole to awake, thy sun-bathed head
     Piercing the solemn cloud
Round thy still dreaming brother-world outspread!
O man, whom Earth, thy long-vext mother, bare
Not without joy, so radiant, so endow'd
(Such happy issue crown'd her painful care)!
     Be not too proud!

Thy native world stirs at thy feet unknown,
    Yet there thy secret lies!
Out of this stuff, these forces, thou art grown,
And proud self-severance from them were disease.
O scan thy native world with pious eyes!
High as thy life be risen, 'tis from these;
    And these, too, rise.

LINES

WRITTEN IN KENSINGTON GARDENS.

IN this lone open glade I lie,
  Screen'd by deep boughs on either hand.
Where ends the glade, to stay the eye
Those black-crown'd, red-boled pine-trees stand !

Birds here make song, each bird has his,
Across the girdling city's hum;
How green under the boughs it is !
How thick the tremulous sheep-cries come !

Sometimes a child will cross the glade
To take his nurse his broken toy;
Sometimes a thrush flit overhead
Deep in her unknown day's employ.

Here at my feet what wonders pass,
What endless, active life is here !
What blowing daisies, fragrant grass !
An air-stirr'd forest, fresh and clear.

Scarce fresher is the mountain-sod
Where the tired angler lies, stretch'd out,
And, eased of basket and of rod,
Counts his day's spoil, the spotted trout.

In the huge world, which roars hard by,
Be others happy if they can!
But in my helpless cradle I
Was breathed on by the rural Pan.

I, on men's impious uproar hurl'd,
Think often, as I hear them rave,
That peace has left the upper world,
And now keeps only in the grave.

Yet here is peace for ever new!
When I who watch them am away,
Still all things in this glade go through
The changes of their quiet day.

Then to their happy rest they pass;
The flowers upclose, the birds are fed,
The night comes down upon the grass,
The child sleeps warmly in his bed.

Calm soul of all things! make it mine
To feel, amid the city's jar,
That there abides a peace of thine,
Man did not make, and cannot mar!

The will to neither strive nor cry,
The power to feel with others give!
Calm, calm me more! nor let me die
Before I have begun to live.

PALLADIUM.

SET where the upper streams of Simois flow
    Was the Palladium, high 'mid rock and wood;
And Hector was in Ilium, far below,
And fought, and saw it not—but there it stood.

It stood, and sun and moonshine rain'd their light
On the pure columns of its glen-built hall.
Backward and forward roll'd the waves of fight
Round Troy; but while this stood, Troy could not fall.

So, in its lovely moonlight, lives the soul!
Mountains surround it, and sweet virgin air;
Cold plashing, past it, crystal waters roll;
We visit it by moments, ah, too rare!

Men will renew the battle in the plain
To-morrow; red with blood will Xanthus be,
Hector and Ajax will be there again,
Helen will come upon the wall to see.

Then we shall rust in shade, or shine in strife,
And fluctuate 'twixt blind hopes and blind despairs,
And fancy that we put forth all our life,
And never know how with the soul it fares.

Still doth the soul, from its lone fastness high,
Upon our life a ruling effluence send;
And when it fails, fight as we will, we die,
And while it lasts, we cannot wholly end.

A WISH.

I ASK not that my bed of death
From bands of greedy heirs be free;
For these besiege the latest breath
Of fortune's favour'd sons, not me.

I ask not each kind soul to keep
Tearless, when of my death he hears;
Let those who will, if any, weep!
There are worse plagues on earth than tears.

I ask but that my death may find
The freedom to my life denied!
Ask but the folly of mankind,
Then, then at last, to quit my side!

Spare me the whispering, crowded room,
The friends who come, and gape, and go;
The ceremonious air of gloom—
All, that makes death a hideous show!

Nor bring, to see me cease to live,
Some doctor full of phrase and fame,
To shake his sapient head, and give
The ill he cannot cure a name!

Nor fetch, to take the accustom'd toll
Of the poor sinner bound for death,
His brother doctor of the soul,
To canvass with official breath

The future and its viewless things—
That undiscover'd mystery
Which one who feels death's winnowing wings
Must needs read clearer, sure, than he!

Bring none of these! but let me be,
While all around in silence lies,
Moved to the window near, and see
Once more, before my dying eyes,

Bathed in the sacred dews of morn
The wide aërial landscape spread—
The world which was ere I was born,
The world which lasts when I am dead!

Which never was the friend of *one*,
Nor promised love it could not give;
But lit for all its generous sun,
And lived itself, and made us live.

There let me gaze, till I become
In soul with what I gaze on wed!
To feel the universe my home;
To have before my mind—instead

Of a sick room, a mortal strife,
A turmoil for a little breath—
The pure eternal course of life,
Not human combatings with death.

Thus feeling, gazing, let me grow
Composed, refresh'd, ennobled, clear;
Then willing let my spirit go
To work or wait elsewhere or here!

CONSOLATION.

MIST clogs the sunshine ;
    Smoky dwarf houses
Hem me round everywhere ;
A vague dejection
Weighs down my soul.

Yet, while I languish,
Everywhere countless
Prospects unroll themselves,
And countless beings
Pass countless moods.

Far hence, in Asia,
On the smooth convent-roofs
On the gold terraces
Of holy Lassa,
Bright shines the sun.

Grey time-worn marbles
Hold the pure Muses;
In their cool gallery,
By yellow Tiber,
They still look fair.

Strange unloved uproar *
Shrills round their portal;
Yet not on Helicon
Kept they more cloudless
Their noble calm.

Through sun-proof alleys
In a lone, sand-hemm'd
City of Africa,
A blind, led beggar,
Age-bow'd, asks alms.

No bolder robber
Erst abode ambush'd
Deep in the sandy waste;
No clearer eyesight
Spied prey afar.

* Written during the siege of Rome by the French.

Saharan sand-winds
Sear'd his keen eyeballs;
Spent is the spoil he won!
For him the present
Holds only pain.

Two young, fair lovers,
Where the warm June-wind,
Fresh from the summer fields,
Plays fondly round them,
Stand, tranced in joy.

With sweet, join'd voices,
And with eyes brimming:
' Ah,' they cry, ' Destiny !
Prolong the present;
Time, stand still here !'

The prompt stern Goddess
Shakes her head, frowning;
Time gives his hour-glass
Its due reversal;
Their hour is gone!

With weak indulgence
Did the just Goddess
Lengthen their happiness,
She lengthen'd also
Distress elsewhere.

The hour, whose happy
Unalloy'd moments
I would eternalise,
Ten thousand mourners
Well pleased see end.

The bleak stern hour,
Whose severe moments
I would annihilate,
Is pass'd by others
In warmth, light, joy.

Time, so complain'd of,
Who to no one man
Shows partiality,
Brings round to all men
Some undimm'd hours.

SELF-DEPENDENCE.

WEARY of myself, and sick of asking
    What I am, and what I ought to be,
At the vessel's prow I stand, which bears me
Forwards, forwards, o'er the starlit sea.

And a look of passionate desire
O'er the sea and to the stars I send:
'Ye who from my childhood up have calm'd me,
Calm me, ah, compose me to the end!

Ah, once more,' I cried, 'ye stars, ye waters,
On my heart your mighty charm renew!
Still, still let me, as I gaze upon you,
Feel my soul becoming vast like you!'

From the intense, clear, star-sown vault of heaven,
Over the lit sea's unquiet way,
In the rustling night-air came the answer:
'Wouldst thou *be* as these are? *Live* as they!

Unaffrighted by the silence round them,
Undistracted by the sights they see,
These demand not, that the things without them
Yield them love, amusement, sympathy.

And with joy the stars perform their shining,
And the sea its long moon-silver'd roll;
Why?—self-poised they live, nor pine with noting
All the fever of some differing soul.

Bounded by themselves, and unregardful
In what state God's other works may be,
In their own tasks all their powers pouring,
These attain the mighty life you see.'

* * * *

O air-born voice! long since, severely clear
A cry like thine in mine own heart I hear:
'Resolve to be thyself! and know, that he
Who finds himself, loses his misery!'

MORALITY.

WE cannot kindle when we will
    The fire which in the heart resides,
The spirit bloweth and is still,
In mystery our soul abides;
    But tasks in hours of insight will'd
    Can be through hours of gloom fulfill'd.

With aching hands and bleeding feet
We dig and heap, lay stone on stone;
We bear the burden and the heat
Of the long day, and wish 'twere done.
    Not till the hours of light return
    All we have built do we discern.

Then, when the clouds are off the soul,
When thou dost bask in Nature's eye,
Ask, how *she* view'd thy self-control,
Thy struggling, task'd morality—
    Nature, whose free, light, cheerful air,
    Oft made thee, in thy gloom, despair.

And she, whose censure thou dost dread,
Whose eye thou wast afraid to seek,
See, on her face a glow is spread,
A strong emotion on her cheek!
   'Ah, child!' she cries, 'that strife divine,
   Whence was it, for it is not mine?

There is no effort on *my* brow—
I do not strive, I do not weep;
I rush with the swift spheres and glow
In joy, and, when I will, I sleep!
   Yet that severe, that earnest air,
   I saw, I felt it once—but where?

I knew not yet the gauge of time,
Nor wore the manacles of space;
I felt it in some other clime!
I saw it in some other place!
   'Twas when the heavenly house I trod,
   And lay upon the breast of God.'

HEINE'S GRAVE.

Henri Heine——'tis here!
The black tombstone, the name
Carved there—no more! and the smooth,
Swarded alleys, the limes
Touch'd with yellow by hot
Summer, but under them still
In September's bright afternoon
Shadow, and verdure, and cool!
Trim Montmartre! the faint
Murmur of Paris outside;
Crisp everlasting-flowers,
Yellow and black, on the graves.

Half blind, palsied, in pain,
Hither to come, from the streets'
Uproar, surely not loath
Wast thou, Heine!—to lie
Quiet! to ask for closed
Shutters, and darken'd room,

And cool drinks, and an eased
Posture, and opium, no more!
Hither to come, and to sleep
Under the wings of Renown.

Ah, not little, when pain
Is most quelling, and man
Easily quell'd, and the fine
Temper of genius alive
Quickest to ill, is the praise
Not to have yielded to pain!
No small boast, for a weak
Son of mankind, to the earth
Pinn'd by the thunder, to rear
His bolt-scathed front to the stars;
And, undaunted, retort
'Gainst thick-crashing, insane,
Tyrannous tempests of bale,
Arrowy lightnings of soul!

Hark! through the alley resounds
Mocking laughter! A film
Creeps o'er the sunshine; a breeze
Ruffles the warm afternoon,

Saddens my soul with its chill!
Gibing of spirits in scorn
Shakes every leaf of the grove,
Mars the benignant repose
Of this amiable home of the dead.

Bitter spirits! ye claim
Heine?——Alas, he is yours!
Only a moment I long'd
Here in the quiet to snatch
From such mates the outworn
Poet, and steep him in calm.
Only a moment! I knew
Whose he was who is here
Buried, I knew he was yours!
Ah, I knew that I saw
Here no sepulchre built
In the laurell'd rock, o'er the blue
Naples bay, for a sweet
Tender Virgil! no tomb
On Ravenna sands, in the shade
Of Ravenna pines, for a high
Austere Dante! no grave
By the Avon side, in the bright

Stratford meadows, for thee,
Shakspeare! loveliest of souls,
Peerless in radiance, in joy!

What so harsh and malign,
Heine! distils from thy life,
Poisons the peace of thy grave?

I chide with thee not, that thy sharp
Upbraidings often assail'd
England, my country; for we,
Troublous and sad, for her sons,
Long since, deep in our hearts,
Echo the blame of her foes.
We, too, sigh that she flags!
We, too, say that she now,
Scarce comprehending the voice
Of her greatest, golden-mouth'd sons
Of a former age any more,
Stupidly travels her round
Of mechanic business, and lets
Slow die out of her life
Glory, and genius, and joy!

So thou arraign'st her, her foe.
So we arraign her, her sons.

Yes, we arraign her! but she,
The weary Titan! with deaf
Ears, and labour-dimm'd eyes,
Regarding neither to right
Nor left, goes passively by,
Staggering on to her goal;
Bearing on shoulders immense,
Atlanteän, the load,
Wellnigh not to be borne,
Of the too vast orb of her fate.

But was it thou—I think
Surely it was—that bard
Unnamed, who, Goethe said,
Had every other gift, but wanted love;
Love, without which the tongue
Even of angels sounds amiss?

Charm is the glory which makes
Song of the poet divine;
Love is the fountain of charm!

How without charm wilt thou draw,
Poet! the world to thy way?
Not by the lightnings of wit!
Not by the thunder of scorn!
These to the world, too, are given;
Wit it possesses, and scorn—
Charm is the poet's alone.
Hollow and dull are the great,
And artists envious, and the mob profane.
We know all this, we know!
Cam'st thou from heaven, O child
Of light! but this to declare?
Alas! to help us forget
Such barren knowledge awhile,
God gave the poet his song

Therefore a secret unrest
Tortured thee, brilliant and bold!
Therefore triumph itself
Tasted amiss to thy soul!
Therefore, with blood of thy foes,
Trickled in silence thine own!
Therefore the victor's heart
Broke on the field of his fame!

Ah ! as of old, from the pomp
Of Italian Milan, the fair
Flower of marble of white
Southern palaces—steps .
Border'd by statues, and walks
Terraced, and orange-bowers
Heavy with fragrance—the blond
German Kaiser full oft

Long'd himself back to the fields,
Rivers, and high-roof'd towns
Of his native Germany; so,
So, how often ! from hot
Paris drawing-rooms, and lamps
Blazing, and brilliant crowds,
Starr'd and jewell'd, of men
Famous, of women the queens
Of dazzling converse, and fumes
Of praise—hot, heady fumes, to the poor brain
That mount, that madden !—how oft
Heine's spirit outworn
Long'd itself out of the din
Back to the tranquil, the cool
Far German home of his youth !

See ! in the May afternoon,
O'er the fresh short turf of the Hartz,
A youth, with the foot of youth,
Heine ! thou climbest again.
Up, through the tall dark firs
Warming their heads in the sun,
Chequering the grass with their shade—
Up, by the stream with its huge
Moss-hung boulders and thin
Musical water half-hid—
Up, o'er the rock-strewn slope,
With the sinking sun, and the air
Chill, and the shadows now
Long on the grey hill-side—
To the stone-roof'd hut at the top.

Or, yet later, in watch
On the roof of the Brocken-tower
Thou standest, gazing ! to see
The broad red sun, over field
Forest and city and spire
And mist-track'd stream of the wide
Wide German land, going down

In a bank of vapours——again
Standest! at nightfall, alone.

Or, next morning, with limbs
Rested by slumber, and heart
Freshen'd and light with the May,
O'er the gracious spurs coming down
Of the Lower Hartz, among oaks
And beechen coverts and copse
Of hazels green in whose depth
Ilse, the fairy transform'd,
In a thousand water-breaks light
Pours her petulant youth—
Climbing the rock which juts
O'er the valley, the dizzily perch'd
Rock! to its iron cross
Once more thou cling'st; to the Cross
Clingest! with smiles, with a sigh.

Goethe, too, had been there.[11]
In the long-past winter he came
To the frozen Hartz, with his soul
Passionate, eager, his youth
All in ferment!—but he

Destined to work and to live
Left it, and thou, alas,
Only to laugh and to die !

But something prompts me : Not thus
Take leave of Heine, not thus
Speak the last word at his grave !
Not in pity, and not
With half censure—with awe
Hail, as it passes from earth
Scattering lightnings, that soul !

The spirit of the world
Beholding the absurdity of men,—
Their vaunts, their feats,—let a sardonic smile,
For one short moment, wander o'er his lips.
That smile was Heine ! for its earthly hour
The strange guest sparkled ; now 'tis pass'd
    away.

That was Heine ! and we,
Myriads who live, who have lived,
What are we all, but a mood,
A single mood, of the life

Of the Being in whom we exist,
Who alone is all things in one.

Spirit, who fillest us all!
Spirit who utterest in each
New-coming son of mankind
Such of thy thoughts as thou wilt!
O thou, one of whose moods,
Bitter and strange, was the life
Of Heine—his strange, alas!
His bitter life – may a life
Other and milder be mine!
May'st thou a mood more serene,
Happier, have utter'd in mine!
May'st thou the rapture of peace
Deep have embreathed at its core!
Made it a ray of thy thought!
Made it a beat of thy joy!

REVOLUTIONS.

BEFORE man parted for this earthly strand,
    While yet upon the verge of heaven he stood,
God put a heap of letters in his hand,
And bade him make with them what word he could.

And man has turn'd them many times; made Greece,
Rome, England, France;—yes, nor in vain essay'd
Way after way, changes that never cease!
The letters have combined; something was made.

But ah, an inextinguishable sense
Haunts him that he has not made what he should!
That he has still, though old, to recommence,
Since he has not yet found the word God would!

And empire after empire, at their height
Of sway, have felt this boding sense come on;
Have felt their huge frames not constructed right,
And droop'd, and slowly died upon their throne.

One day, thou say'st, there will at last appear
The word, the order, which God meant should be.
—Ah, we shall know *that* well when it comes near!
The band will quit man's heart; he will breathe free.

STANZAS FROM

THE GRANDE CHARTREUSE.

THROUGH Alpine meadows soft suffused
   With rain, where thick the crocus blows,
Past the dark forges long disused,
The mule-track from Saint Laurent goes.
The bridge is cross'd, and slow we ride,
Through forest, up the mountain-side.

The autumnal evening darkens round,
The wind is up, and drives the rain ;
While hark ! far down, with strangled sound
Doth the Dead Guier's stream complain,
Where that wet smoke among the woods
Over his boiling cauldron broods.

Swift rush the spectral vapours white
Past limestone scars with ragged pines,
Showing—then blotting from our sight.

Halt! through the cloud-drift something shines!
High in the valley, wet and drear,
The huts of Courrerie appear.

Strike leftward! cries our guide; and higher
Mounts up the stony forest-way.
At last the encircling trees retire;
Look! through the showery twilight grey
What pointed roofs are these advance?—
A palace of the Kings of France?

Approach, for what we seek is here!
Alight, and sparely sup, and wait
For rest in this outbuilding near;
Then cross the sward and reach that gate;
Knock; pass the wicket! Thou art come
To the Carthusians' world-famed home.

The silent courts, where night and day
Into their stone-carved basins cold
The splashing icy fountains play;
The humid corridors behold,
Where ghostlike in the deepening night
Cowl'd forms brush by in gleaming white!

The chapel, where no organ's peal
Invests the stern and naked prayer !
With penitential cries they kneel
And wrestle ; rising then, with bare
And white uplifted faces stand,
Passing the Host from hand to hand ;

Each takes, and then his visage wan
Is buried in his cowl once more.
The cells—the suffering Son of Man
Upon the wall ! the knee-worn floor !
And where they sleep, that wooden bed,
Which shall their coffin be, when dead !

The library, where tract and tome
Not to feed priestly pride are there,
To hymn the conquering march of Rome,
Nor yet to amuse, as worldlings' are !
They paint of souls the inner strife,
Their drops of blood, their death in life.

The garden, overgrown—yet mild
Those fragrant herbs are flowering there !
Strong children of the Alpine wild

Whose culture is the brethren's care;
Of human tasks their only one,
And cheerful works beneath the sun.

Those halls too, destined to contain
Each its own pilgrim-host of old,
From England, Germany, or Spain—
All are before me! I behold
The House, the Brotherhood austere!—
And what am I, that I am here?

For rigorous teachers seized my youth,
And purged its faith, and trimm'd its fire,
Shew'd me the high white star of Truth,
There bade me gaze, and there aspire.
Even now their whispers pierce the gloom:
What dost thou in this living tomb?

Forgive me, masters of the mind!
At whose behest I long ago
So much unlearnt, so much resign'd!
I come not here to be your foe.
I seek these anchorites, not in ruth,
To curse and to deny your truth!

Not as their friend or child I speak !
But as, on some far northern strand,
Thinking of his own Gods, a Greek
In pity and mournful awe might stand
Before some fallen Runic stone—
For both were faiths, and both are gone !

Wandering between two worlds, one dead,
The other powerless to be born,
With nowhere yet to rest my head,
Like these, on earth I wait forlorn.
Their faith, my tears, the world deride;
I come to shed them at their side.

Oh, hide me in your gloom profound
Ye solemn seats of holy pain !
Take me, cowl'd forms, and fence me round,
Till I possess my soul again !
Till free my thoughts before me roll,
Not chafed by hourly false control.

For the world cries your faith is now
But a dead time's exploded dream;
My melancholy, sciolists say,

Is a pass'd mode, an outworn theme—
As if the world had ever had
A faith, or sciolists been sad !

   Ah, if it *be* pass'd, take away,
At least, the restlessness—the pain !
Be man henceforth no more a prey
To these out-dated stings again !
The nobleness of grief is gone —
Ah, leave us not the fret alone !

But, if you cannot give us ease,
Last of the race of them who grieve
Here leave us to die out with these
Last of the people who believe !
Silent, while years engrave the brow;
Silent—the best are silent now.

Achilles ponders in his tent,
The kings of modern thought are dumb;
Silent they are, though not content,
And wait to see the future come.
They have the grief men had of yore,
But they contend and cry no more.

Our fathers water'd with their tears
This sea of time whereon we sail;
Their voices were in all men's ears
Who pass'd within their puissant hail.
Still the same ocean round us raves,
But we stand mute and watch the waves.

For what avail'd it, all the noise
And outcry of the former men?—
Say, have their sons obtain'd more joys?
Say, is life¸lighter now than then?
The sufferers died, they left their pain;
The pangs which tortured them remain!

What helps it now, that Byron bore,
With haughty scorn which mock'd the smart,
Through Europe to the Ætolian shore
The pageant of his bleeding heart?
That thousands counted every groan,
And Europe made his woe her own?

What boots it, Shelley! that the breeze
Carried thy lovely wail away,
Musical through Italian trees

Which fringe thy soft blue Spezzian bay?
Inheritors of thy distress
Have restless hearts one throb the less?

Or are we easier, to have read,
O Obermann! the sad, stern page,
Which tells us how thou hidd'st thy head
From the fierce tempest of thine age
In the lone brakes of Fontainebleau,
Or chalets near the Alpine snow?

Ye slumber in your silent grave!
The world, which for an idle day
Grace to your mood of sadness gave,
Long since hath flung her weeds away.
The eternal trifler breaks your spell;
But we—we learnt your lore too well!

There yet, perhaps, may dawn an age,
More fortunate, alas! than we,
Which without hardness will be sage,
And gay without frivolity.
Sons of the world, oh, haste those years;
But, till they rise, allow our tears!

Allow them! We admire with awe
The exulting thunder of your race;
You give the universe your law,
You triumph over time and space.
Your pride of life, your tireless powers,
We mark them, but they are not ours.

We are like children rear'd in shade
Beneath some old-world abbey-wall,
Forgotten in a forest-glade,
And secret from the eyes of all.
Deep, deep the greenwood round them waves,
Their abbey, and its close of graves!

But where the road runs near the stream,
Oft through the trees they catch a glance
Of passing troops in the sun's beam—
Pennon, and plume, and flashing lance!
Forth to the world those soldiers fare,
To life, to cities, and to war.

And through the woods, another way,
Faint bugle-notes from far are borne,
Where hunters gather, staghounds bay,

Round some old forest-lodge at morn.
Gay dames are there in sylvan green,
Laughter and cries—those notes between!

The banners flashing through the trees
Make their blood dance and chain their eyes;
That bugle-music on the breeze
Arrests them with a charm'd surprise.
Banner by turns and bugle woo:
Ye shy recluses, follow too!

O children, what do ye reply?—
'Action and pleasure, will ye roam
Through these secluded dells to cry
And call us? but too late ye come!
Too late for us your call ye blow,
Whose bent was taken long ago.

Long since we pace this shadow'd nave;
We watch those yellow tapers shine,
Emblems of hope over the grave,
In the high altar's depth divine.
The organ carries to our ear
Its accents of another sphere.

Fenced early in this cloistral round
Of reverie, of shade, of prayer,
How should we grow in other ground?
How should we flower in foreign air?—
Pass, banners, pass, and bugles, cease!
And leave our desert to its peace!'

PROGRESS.

THE Master stood upon the mount, and taught.
  He saw a fire in his disciples' eyes;
'The old law,' they said, 'is wholly come to nought!
  Behold the new world rise!'

'Was it,' the Lord then said, 'with scorn ye saw
The old law observed by Scribes and Pharisees?
I say unto you, see *ye* keep that law
  More faithfully than these!

Too hasty heads for ordering worlds, alas!
Think not that I to annul the law have will'd;
No jot, no tittle from the law shall pass,
  Till all hath been fulfill'd.'

So Christ said eighteen hundred years ago.
And what then shall be said to those to-day
Who cry aloud to lay the old world low
  To clear the new world's way?

'Religious fervours! ardour misapplied!
Hence, hence,' they cry, 'ye do but keep man blind!
But keep him self-immersed, preoccupied,
    And lame the active mind.'

Ah! from the old world let some one answer give:
'Scorn ye this world, their tears, their inward cares?
I say unto you, see that *your* souls live
    A deeper life than theirs.

Say ye: 'The spirit of man has found new roads,
And we must leave the old faiths, and walk therein?'—
Leave then the Cross as ye have left carved gods,
    But guard the fire within!

Bright, else, and fast the stream of life may roll,
And no man may the other's hurt behold;
Yet each will have one anguish!—his own soul
    Which perishes of cold.'

Here let that voice make end; then, let a strain
From a far lonelier distance, like the wind
Be heard, floating through heaven, and fill again
    These men's profoundest mind:

'Children of men! the unseen Power, whose eye
For ever doth accompany mankind,
Hath look'd on no religion scornfully
      That men did ever find.

Which has not taught weak wills how much they can?
Which has not fall'n on the dry heart like rain?
Which has not cried to sunk, self-weary man:
      Thou must be born again!

Children of men! not that your age excel
In pride of life the ages of your sires,
But that you think clear, feel deep, bear fruit well,
      The Friend of man desires.'

STANZAS

IN MEMORY OF THE AUTHOR OF

OBERMANN.[12]

IN front the awful Alpine track
  Crawls up its rocky stair;
The autumn storm-winds drive the rack,
Close o'er it, in the air.

Behind are the abandon'd baths [13]
Mute in their meadows lone;
The leaves are on the valley paths,
The mists are on the Rhone—

The white mists rolling like a sea!
I hear the torrents roar.
—Yes, Obermann, all speaks of thee;
I feel thee near once more!

I turn thy leaves! I feel their breath
Once more upon me roll;
That air of languor, cold, and death,
Which brooded o'er thy soul.

Fly hence, poor wretch, whoe'er thou art,
Condemn'd to cast about,
All shipwreck in thy own weak heart,
For comfort from without!

A fever in these pages burns
Beneath the calm they feign;
A wounded human spirit turns,
Here, on its bed of pain.

Yes, though the virgin mountain air
Fresh through these pages blows,
Though to these leaves the glaciers spare
The soul of their white snows;

Though here a mountain-murmur swells
Of many a dark-bough'd pine,
Though, as you read, you hear the bells
Of the high-pasturing kine—

Yet, through the hum of torrent lone,
And brooding mountain-bee,
There sobs I know not what ground-tone
Of human agony!

Is it for this, because the sound
Is fraught too deep with pain,
That, Obermann! the world around
So little loves thy strain?

Some secrets may the poet tell,
For the world loves new ways;
To tell too deep ones is not well—
It knows not what he says.

Yet of the spirits who have reign'd
In this our troubled day,
I know but two, who have attain'd,
Save thee, to see their way.

By England's lakes, in grey old age,
His quiet home one keeps; *
And one, the strong much-toiling sage,
In German Weimar sleeps.

But Wordsworth's eyes avert their ken
From half of human fate;
And Goethe's course few sons of men
May think to emulate.

* Written in November, 1849.

For he pursued a lonely road,
His eyes on Nature's plan;
Neither made man too much a God,
Nor God too much a man.

Strong was he, with a spirit free
From mists, and sane, and clear;
Clearer, how much! than ours—yet we
Have a worse course to steer.

For though his manhood bore the blast
Of a tremendous time,
Yet in a tranquil world was pass'd
His tenderer youthful prime.

But we, brought forth and rear'd in hours
Of change, alarm, surprise—
What shelter to grow ripe is ours?
What leisure to grow wise?

Like children bathing on the shore,
Buried a wave beneath,
The second wave succeeds, before
We have had time to breathe.

Too fast we live, too much are tried,
Too harass'd, to attain
Wordsworth's sweet calm, or Goethe's wide
And luminous view to gain.

And then we turn, thou sadder sage,
To thee! we feel thy spell!—
The hopeless tangle of our age,
Thou too hast scann'd it well!

Immoveable thou sittest, still
As death, composed to bear;
Thy head is clear, thy feeling chill,
And icy thy despair.

Yes, as the son of Thetis said,
One hears thee saying now:
Greater by far than thou are dead;
Strive not! die also thou.

Ah, two desires toss about
The poet's feverish blood!
One drives him to the world without,
And one to solitude.

The glow, he cries, *the thrill of life !*
Where, where do these abound ?—
Not in the world, not in the strife
Of men, shall they be found.

He who hath watch'd, not shared, the strife,
Knows how the day hath gone;
He only lives with the world's life
Who hath renounced his own.

To thee we come, then,   Clouds are roll'd
Where thou, O seer, art set;
Thy realm of thought is drear and cold—
The world is colder yet !

And thou hast pleasures, too, to share
With those who come to thee !
Balms floating on thy mountain-air,
And healing sights to see.

How often, where the slopes are green
On Jaman, hast thou sate
By some high chalet-door, and seen
The summer day grow late,

And darkness steal o'er the wet grass
With the pale crocus starr'd,
And reach that glimmering sheet of glass
Beneath the piny sward,

Lake Leman's waters, far below!
And watch'd the rosy light
Fade from the distant peaks of snow;
And on the air of night

Heard accents of the eternal tongue
Through the pine branches play!
Listen'd, and felt thyself grow young!
Listen'd, and wept——Away!

Away the dreams that but deceive!
And thou, sad guide, adieu!
I go; fate drives me! but I leave
Half of my life with you.

We, in some unknown Power's employ,
Move on a rigorous line;
Can neither, when we will, enjoy,
Nor, when we will, resign.

I in the world must live! but thou,
Thou melancholy shade,
Wilt not, if thou can'st see me now,
Condemn me, nor upbraid!

For thou art gone away from earth,
And place with those dost claim,
The children of the second birth
Whom the world could not tame;

And with that small transfigured band,
Whom many a different way
Conducted to their common land,
Thou learn'st to think as they.

Christian and pagan, king and slave,
Soldier and anchorite,
Distinctions we esteem so grave,
Are nothing in their sight.

They do not ask, who pined unseen,
Who was on action hurl'd,
Whose one bond is, that all have been
Unspotted by the world.

There without anger thou wilt see
Him who obeys thy spell
No more, so he but rest, like thee,
Unsoil'd;—and so, farewell!

Farewell!—Whether thou now liest near
That much-loved inland sea
The ripples of whose blue waves cheer
Vevey and Meillerie;

And in that gracious region bland,
Where with clear-rustling wave
The scented pines of Switzerland
Stand dark round thy green grave,

Between the dusty vineyard-walls
Issuing on that green place
The early peasant still recalls
The pensive stranger's face,

And stoops to clear thy moss-grown date
Ere he plods on again;—
Or whether, by maligner fate,
Among the swarms of men,

Where between granite terraces
The blue Seine rolls her wave,
The capital of pleasure sees
Thy hardly-heard-of grave—

Farewell! Under the sky we part,
In this stern Alpine dell.
O unstrung will! O broken heart
A last, a last farewell!

OBERMANN ONCE MORE.

(COMPOSED MANY YEARS AFTER THE PRECEDING.)

Savez-vous quelque bien qui console du regret d'un monde ?
OBERMANN.

GLION ?——Ah, twenty years, it cuts [14]
   All meaning from a name !
White houses prank where once were huts ;
Glion, but not the same !

And yet I know not ! All unchanged
   The turf, the pines, the sky ;
The hills in their old order ranged ;
   The lake, with Chillon by !

And 'neath those chestnut-trees, where stiff
   And stony mounts the way,
Their crackling husk-heaps burn, as if
   I left them yesterday.

Across the valley, on that slope,
   The huts of Avant shine !
Its pines under their branches ope
   Ways for the tinkling kine.

Full-foaming milk-pails, Alpine fare,
Sweet heaps of fresh-cut grass,
Invite to rest the traveller there
Before he climb the pass—

The gentian-flower'd pass, its crown[15]
With yellow spires aflame;
Whence drops the path to Allière down,
And walls where Byron came,[16]

By their green river who doth change
His birth-name just below—
Orchard, and croft, and full-stored grange
Nursed by his pastoral flow.

But stop!—to fetch back thoughts that stray
Beyond this gracious bound,
The cone of Jaman, pale and grey,
See, in the blue profound!

Ah, Jaman! delicately tall
Above his sun-warm'd firs—
What thoughts to me his rocks recall!
What memories he stirs!

And who but thou must be, in truth,
Obermann! with me here?
Thou master of my wandering youth,
But left this many a year!

Yes, I forget the world's work wrought,
Its warfare waged with pain!
An eremite with thee, in thought
Once more I slip my chain,

And to thy mountain-chalet come,
And lie beside its door;
And hear the wild bee's Alpine hum,
And thy sad, tranquil lore!

Again I feel its words inspire
Their mournful calm—serene,
Yet tinged with infinite desire
For all that *might* have been;

The harmony from which man swerved
Made his life's rule once more!
The universal order served!
Earth happier than before!

While thus I mused, night gently ran
Down over hill and wood.
Then, still and sudden, Obermann
On the grass near me stood.

Those pensive features well I knew,
On my mind, years before,
Imaged so oft, imaged so true!
A shepherd's garb he wore,

A mountain-flower was in his hand,
A book was in his breast;
Bent on my face, with gaze which scann'd
My soul, his eyes did rest.

'And is it thou,' he cried, 'so long
Held by the world which we
Loved not, who turnest from the throng
Back to thy youth and me?

And from thy world, with heart opprest,
Choosest thou *now* to turn?—
Ah me, we anchorites knew it best!
Best can its course discern!

Thou fledd'st me when the ungenial earth,
Thou soughtest, lay in gloom;—
Return'st thou in her hour of birth,
Of hopes and hearts in bloom?

Wellnigh two thousand years have brought
Their load, and gone away,
Since last on earth there lived and wrought
A world like ours to-day.

Like ours it look'd in outward air!
But of that inward prize,
Soul, that we take more count and care,
Ah! there our future lies.

Like ours it look'd in outward air!—
Its head was clear and true,
Sumptuous its clothing, rich its fare,
No pause its action knew;

Stout was its arm, each thew and bone
Seem'd puissant and alive—
But, ah! its heart, its heart was stone,
And so it could not thrive.

On that hard Pagan world disgust
And secret loathing fell;
Deep weariness and sated lust
Made human life a hell.

In his cool hall, with haggard eyes,
The Roman noble lay;
He drove abroad, in furious guise,
Along the Appian way;

He made a feast, drank fierce and fast,
And crown'd his hair with flowers—
No easier nor no quicker pass'd
The impracticable hours.

The brooding East with awe beheld
Her impious younger world.
The Roman tempest swell'd and swell'd,
And on her head was hurl'd.

The East bow'd low before the blast
In patient, deep disdain;
She let the legions thunder past,
And plunged in thought again.

So well she mused, a morning broke
Across her spirit grey.
A conquering, new-born joy awoke,
And fill'd her life with day.

"Poor world," she cried, "so deep accurst!
That runn'st from pole to pole
To seek a draught to slake thy thirst—
Go, seek it in thy soul!"

She heard it, the victorious West,
In crown and sword array'd!
She felt the void which mined her breast,
She shiver'd and obey'd.

She veil'd her eagles, snapp'd her sword,
And laid her sceptre down;
Her stately purple she abhorr'd,
And her imperial crown;

She broke her flutes, she stopp'd her sports,
Her artists could not please;
She tore her books, she shut her courts,
She fled her palaces.

Lust of the eye and pride of life
She left it all behind—
And hurried, torn with inward strife,
The wilderness to find.

Tears wash'd the trouble from her face!
She changed into a child!
'Mid weeds and wrecks she stood—a place
Of ruin—but she smiled!

Oh, had I lived in that great day,
How had its glory new
Fill'd earth and heaven, and caught away
My ravish'd spirit too!

No cloister-floor of humid stone
Had been too cold for me;
For me no Eastern desert lone
Had been too far to flee.

No thoughts that to the world belong
Had stood against the wave
Of love which set so deep and strong
From Christ's then open grave.

No lonely life had pass'd too slow
When I could hourly see
That wan, nail'd Form, with head droop'd low,
Upon the bitter tree;

Could see the Mother with the Child
Whose tender winning arts
Have to his little arms beguiled
So many wounded hearts!

And centuries came, and ran their course,
And unspent all that time
·Still, still went forth that Child's dear force,
And still was at its prime.

Ay, ages long endured his span
Of life, 'tis true received,
That gracious Child, that thorn-crown'd Man!
He lived while we believed.

While we believed, on earth he went,
And open stood his grave;
Men call'd from chamber, church, and tent,
And Christ was by to save.

Now he is dead! Far hence he lies
In the lorn Syrian town,
And on his grave, with shining eyes,
The Syrian stars look down.

In vain men still, with hoping new,
Regard his death-place dumb,
And say the stone is not yet to,
And wait for words to come.

Ah, from that silent sacred land,
Of sun, and arid stone,
And crumbling wall, and sultry sand,
Comes now one word alone!

From David's lips this word did roll,
'Tis true and living yet:
No man can save his brother's soul,
Nor pay his brother's debt.

Alone, self-poised, henceforward man
Must labour! must resign
His all too human creeds, and scan
Simply the way divine.

But slow that tide of common thought,
Which bathed our life, retired;
Slow, slow the old world wore to nought,
And pulse by pulse expired.

Its frame yet stood without a breach
When blood and warmth were fled;
And still it spake its wonted speech—
But every word was dead.

And oh, we cried, that on this corse
Might fall a freshening storm !
·Rive its dry bones, and with new force
A new-sprung world inform !

Down came the storm ! O'er France it pass'd
In sheets of scathing fire.
All Europe felt that fiery blast,
And shook as it rush'd by her.

Down came the storm ! In ruins fell
The outworn world we knew.
It pass'd, that elemental swell !
Again appear'd the blue.

The sun shone in the new-wash'd sky—
And what from heaven saw he?
Blocks of the past, like icebergs high,
Float on a rolling sea!

Upon them ply the race of man
All they before endeavour'd;
They come and go, they work and plan,
And know not they are sever'd!

Poor fragments of a broken world
Whereon we pitch our tent!
Why were ye, too, to death not hurl'd
When your world's day was spent?

That glow of central fire is done
Which with its fusing flame
Knit all your parts, and kept you one;—
But ye, ye are the same!

The past, its mask of union on,
Had ceased to live and thrive;
The past, its mask of union gone,
Say, is it more alive?

Your creeds are dead, your rites are dead,
Your social order too !
Where tarries he, the Power who said :
See, I make all things new ?

The millions suffer still, and grieve—
And what can helpers heal
With old-world cures men half believe
For woes they wholly feel?

And yet they have such need of joy !
And joy whose grounds are true,
And joy that should all hearts employ
As when the past was new !

Ah, not the emotion of that past,
Its common hope, were vain !
A new such hope must dawn at last,
Or man must toss in pain.

But now the past is out of date,
The future not yet born—
And who can be *alone* elate,
While the world lies forlorn ?

Then to the wilderness I fled.
There among Alpine snows
And pastoral huts I hid my head,
And sought and found repose.

It was not yet the appointed hour!
Sad, patient, and resign'd,
I watch'd the crocus fade and flower,
I felt the sun and wind.

The day I lived in was not mine;
Man gets no second day.
In dreams I saw the future shine,
But, ah, I could not stay!

Action I had not, followers, fame;
I pass'd obscure, alone!
The after-world forgets my name,
Nor do I wish it known.

Gloom-wrapt within, I lived and died,
And knew my life was vain.
Whith fate I murmur not, nor chide!
At Sèvres by the Seine

(If Paris that brief flight allow)
My humble tomb explore;
It bears: *Eternity, be thou
My refuge!* and no more.

But thou, whom fellowship of mood
Did make from haunts of strife
Come to my mountain-solitude
And learn my frustrate life;

O thou, who, ere thy flying span
Was past of cheerful youth,
Didst seek the solitary man
And love his cheerless truth—

Despair not thou as I despair'd,
Nor be cold gloom thy prison!
Forward the gracious hours have fared,
And see! the sun is risen.

He melts the icebergs of the past,
A green, new earth appears!
Millions, whose life in ice lay fast,
Have thoughts, and smiles, and tears.

The world's great order dawns in sheen
After long darkness rude,
Divinelier imaged, clearer seen,
With happier zeal pursued.

With hope extinct and brow composed
I mark'd the present die;
Its term of life was nearly closed,
Yet it had more than I.

But thou, though to the world's new hour
Thou come with aspect marr'd,
Shorn of the joy, the bloom, the power,
Which best beseem its bard;

Though more than half thy years be past,
And spent thy youthful prime;
Though, round thy firmer manhood cast,
Hang weeds of our sad time,

Whereof thy youth felt all the spell,
And traversed all the shade—
Though late, though dimm'd, though weak, yet tell
Hope to a world re-made!

Help it to reach our deep desire,
The dream which fill'd our brain,
Fix'd in our soul a thirst like fire,
Immedicable pain!

Which to the wilderness drove out
Our life, to Alpine snow;
And palsied all our deed with doubt,
And all our word with woe!

What still of strength is left, employ,
That end to help men gain:
One mighty wave of thought and joy
Lifting mankind amain!'

The vision ended! I awoke
As out of sleep, and no
Voice moved—only the torrent broke
The silence, far below.

Soft darkness on the turf did lie;
Solemn, o'er hut and wood,
In the yet star-sown nightly sky,
The peak of Jaman stood.

Still in my soul the voice I heard
Of Obermann!——away
I turned; by some vague impulse stirr'd,
Along the rocks of Naye

And Sonchaud's piny flanks I gaze,
And the blanch'd summit bare
Of Malatrait, to where in haze
The Valais opens fair,

And the domed Velan, with his snows,
Behind the upcrowding hills,
Doth all the heavenly opening close
Which the Rhone's murmur fills;

And glorious there, without a sound,
Across the glimmering lake,
High in the Valais-depth profound,
I saw the morning break.

THE FUTURE.

A WANDERER is man from his birth.
He was born in a ship
On the breast of the river of Time;
Brimming with wonder and joy
He spreads out his arms to the light,
Rivets his gaze on the banks of the stream.

As what he sees is, so have his thoughts been.
Whether he wakes
Where the snowy mountainous pass,
Echoing the screams of the eagles,
Hems in its gorges the bed
Of the new-born clear-flowing stream;
Whether he first sees light
Where the river in gleaming rings
Sluggishly winds through the plain;
Whether in sound of the swallowing sea—
As is the world on the banks,
So is the mind of the man.

Vainly does each as he glides
Fable and dream
Of the lands which the river of Time ·
Had left ere he woke on its breast,
Or shall reach when his eyes have been closed.
Only the tract where he sails
He wots of; only the thoughts,
Raised by the objects he passes, are his.

Who can see the green earth any more
As she was by the sources of Time?
Who imagines her fields as they lay
In the sunshine, unworn by the plough?
Who thinks as they thought,
The tribes who then roam'd on her breast,   ·
Her vigorous primitive sons?

What girl
Now reads in her bosom as clear
As Rebekah read, when she sate
At eve by the palm-shaded well?
Who guards in her breast
As deep, as pellucid a spring
Of feeling, as tranquil, as sure?

THE FUTURE.

259

What bard,
At the height of his vision, can deem
Of God, of the world, of the soul,
With a plainness as near,
As flashing as Moses felt,
When he lay in the night by his flock
On the starlit Arabian waste?
Can rise and obey
The beck of the Spirit like him?

This tract which the river of Time
Now flows through with us, is the plain.
Gone is the calm of its earlier shore.
Border'd by cities, and hoarse
With a thousand cries is its stream.
And we on its breast, our minds
Are confused as the cries which we hear,
Changing and shot as the sights which we see.

And we say that repose has fled
For ever the course of the river of Time.
That cities will crowd to its edge
In a blacker incessanter line;
That the din will be more on its banks,

S 2

Denser the trade on its stream,
Flatter the plain where it flows,
Fiercer the sun overhead.
That never will those on its breast
See an ennobling sight,
Drink of the feeling of quiet again.

But what was before us we know not,
And we know not what shall succeed.

Haply, the river of Time,
As it grows, as the towns on its marge
Fling their wavering lights
On a wider, statelier stream—
May acquire, if not the calm
Of its early mountainous shore,
Yet a solemn peace of its own.

And the width of the waters, the hush
Of the grey expanse where he floats,
Freshening its current and spotted with foam
As it draws to the Ocean, may strike
Peace to the soul of the man on its breast;
As the pale waste widens around him—

As the banks fade dimmer away—
As the stars come out, and the night-wind
Brings up the stream
Murmurs and scents of the infinite Sea.

NOTES.

NOTE 1, PAGE 12.

Of the sun-loving gentian, in the heat.

The *gentiana lutea.*

NOTE 2, PAGE 49.

Ye Sun-born Virgins ! on the road of truth.

See the Fragments of Parmenides :

. . . . . . κοῦραι δ' ὁδὸν ἡγεμόνευον,
ἡλίαδες κοῦραι, προλιποῦσαι δώματα νυκτός,
εἰς φάος . . . .

NOTE 3, PAGE 64.

The Hunter of the Tanagræan Field.

Orion, the Wild Huntsman of Greek legend, and in this capacity appearing in both earth and sky.

NOTE 4, PAGE 65.

O'er the sun-redden'd western straits.

Erytheia, the legendary region around the Pillars of Hercules, probably took its name from the redness of the West under which the Greeks saw it.

NOTE 5, PAGE 116.

Saw The Wide Prospect, and the Asian Fen.

The name Europe (Εὐρώπη, *the wide prospect*) probably describes the appearance of the European coast to the Greeks on the coast of Asia Minor opposite. The name Asia, again, comes, it has been thought, from the fens of the marshy rivers of Asia Minor, such as the Cayster or Mæander, which struck the imagination of the Greeks living near them.

NOTE 6, PAGE 123.

That son of Italy who tried to blow.

Giacopone di Todi.

NOTE 7, PAGE 127.

Of that unpitying Phrygian sect which cried.

The Montanists.

NOTE 8, PAGE 128.

Recalls the obscure opposer he outweigh'd.

Gilbert de la Porrée, at the Council of Rheims, in 1148.

NOTE 9, PAGE 130.

See St. Augustine's *Confessions*, book ix. chapter 11.

NOTE 10, PAGE 134.

That wayside inn we left to-day.

Those who have been long familiar with the English Lake-Country will have no difficulty in recalling, from the description in the text, the roadside inn at Wythburn on the descent from Dunmail Raise towards Keswick; its sedentary landlord of twenty years ago, and the passage over the Wythburn Fells to Watendlath.

NOTE 11, PAGE 210.

Goethe, too, had been there.

See *Harzreise im Winter*, in Goethe's *Gedichte*.

NOTE 12, PAGE 229.

The author of *Obermann*, Étienne Pivert de Senancour, has little celebrity in France, his own country; and out of France he is almost unknown. But the profound inwardness, the austere sincerity, of his principal work, *Obermann*, the delicate feeling for nature which it exhibits, and the melancholy eloquence of many passages of it, have attracted and charmed some of the most remarkable spirits of this century, such as George Sand and Sainte-Beuve, and will probably always find a certain number of spirits whom they will touch and interest.

Senancour was born in 1770. He was educated for the priesthood, and passed some time in the Seminary of St. Sulpice; broke away from the Seminary and from France itself, and passed some years in Switzerland, where he married; returned to France in middle life, and followed thenceforward the career of a man of letters, but with hardly any fame or success. He died an old man in 1846, desiring that on his grave might be placed these words only : *Éternité, deviens mon asile !*

The influence of Rousseau, and certain affinities with more famous and fortunate authors of his own day,— Chateaubriand and Madame de Staël,—are everywhere visible in Senancour. But though, like these eminent personages, he may be called a sentimental writer, and though *Obermann*, a collection of letters from Switzerland treating almost entirely of nature and of the human soul, may be called a work of sentiment, Senancour has a gravity and severity which distinguish him from all other writers of the sentimental school. The world is with him in his solitude far less than it is with them; of all writers he is the most perfectly isolated and the least attitudinising. His chief work, too, has a value and power of its own, apart from these merits of its author. The stir of all the main forces by which modern life is and has been impelled lives in the letters of *Obermann;* the dissolving agencies of the eighteenth century, the fiery storm of the French Revolution, the first faint promise and dawn of that new world which our own time is but now fully bringing to light,—all these are to be felt, almost to be touched, there. To me, indeed, it will always seem that the impressiveness of this production can hardly be rated too high.

Besides *Obermann* there is one other of Senancour's works which, for those spirits who feel his attraction, is very interesting; its title is, *Libres Méditations d'un Solitaire Inconnu.*

NOTE 13, PAGE 229.

Behind are the abandon'd baths.

The Baths of Leuk. This poem was conceived, and partly composed, in the valley going down from the foot of the Gemmi Pass towards the Rhone.

NOTE 14, PAGE 239.

Glion?—Ah, twenty years, it cuts.

Probably all who know the Vevey end of the Lake of Geneva will recollect Glion, the mountain-village above the castle of Chillon. Glion now has hotels, *pensions*, and villas ; but twenty years ago it was hardly more than the huts of Avant opposite to it,—huts through which goes that beautiful path over the Col de Jaman, followed by so many foot-travellers on their way from Vevey to the Simmenthal and Thun.

NOTE 15, PAGE 240.

The gentian-flower'd pass, its crown.

See Note 1.

NOTE 16, PAGE 240.

And walls where Byron came.

Montbovon. See Byron's Journal, in his *Works*, vol. iii· p. 258. The river Saane becomes the Sarine below Montbovon.